WHISKEY AND SWEET TEA

STRONG INDEPENDENT WOMEN SERIES #3

TIERNEY JAMES

Publishing Coordinator – Sharon Kizziah-Holmes
Cover Design by Sweet 'N Spicy Designs

L & D
PRESS

Owasso, OK

ISBN – 978-1-965460-46-7 (Paperback)
ISBN – 978-1-965460-47-4 (eBook)

DEDICATION

Many thanks to Mary Pat Kelly Tierney for helping me with everything from gunshot wounds to saving the life of the president. My characters appreciate it and so do I.

ACKNOWLEDGMENTS

Sharon Kizziah Holmes & Paperback Press – With each project she is there to weave her magic and put the final book together for me. She is also my main hand holder as the day draws near to pull the trigger and publish.

Decadent Publishing Editors – Kate Richards and Nan Bauserman continue to make me a better writer and give me the encouragement to keep creating. These ladies have been with me almost from the beginning and I hope they will be on my team forever.

Jaycee DeLorenzo Sweet & Spicy Designs – This is always one worry I never have to anticipate because Jaycee knows how to read me and the characters that keep me up at night. She continues to create beautiful covers and never tires of me asking too many questions.

Lipstick & Danger Street Team – These folks help me get the word out and volunteer to be ARC readers when called upon. You guys are my knights in shining armor.

Beta Readers – A big shout out to Becky Young, and Gayle Bodenhamer for taking their time to find the potholes of my story, then building me up with confidence to keep going.

Proofreader – Author Shirley McCann uses her skills like a heat seeking missile to find the little things I missed.

PROLOGUE

Two days into the nightmare

Kade could smell the heat, maybe burning, as he lifted the hood of the seen-better-days pickup. Smoke and steam hissed upward. He and Rasheed tried to fan the area clear, but it belched a cloud of smoke followed by fingers of fire clawing their way to engulf the engine.

"Get out," he yelled, running to the passenger side. He reached in and dragged Vivian to the ground. It barely registered with him that she carried his guitar in hand. Returning to help Rasheed rescue his family, flames now spread beneath the truck. The children wailed in terror as the adults scooped them free of the truck. "Run!" Kade demanded. "We need to get away before it explodes."

Ten seconds later, an explosion rocked the night. Hopefully, the military would be able to locate them before their captors.

How long would it be before the Taliban found them

and made them pay for their disobedience? Rasheed would be executed in front of his family for sure. What consequences did he and Vivian face for the attempted escape? Could he barter for their freedom if they knew how much he was worth? In reality, Vivian's worth surpassed his millions. She could save lives. The only ace he held at the moment was a scratched-up guitar and a song. His self-worth tanked. The realization that all the awards, hit records, and music skills were worthless in this godforsaken land, hit him in the gut. For the first time in his life, it dawned on him how worthless he was in this situation.

War had a way of teaching you what was important and could put you in your place faster than a speeding bullet inscribed with your name.

CHAPTER 1

The sun turned bloodred before sunset as Major Vivian Palmer scrubbed up for surgery. "Who is this character?" she asked the nurse who had slipped on her surgical gloves.

"Kade Atwood. You know, the country music singer? Performer of the year. Best album and best—"

"Got it. He can sing. Why is he here in the middle of a war zone?"

"Entertains the troops. Morale builder. He does it at least once a year. Wrote the patriotic song people choose to sing on political campaigns."

"Oh yeah. Gotcha. I don't listen to country music."

"Bite your tongue," the nurse said then cringed as the major narrowed her focus on her. "Sorry, ma'am. But the world loves Kade Atwood. He's pretty easy on the eyes too."

This caused the major to grin. "Well why didn't you say so. I've been a little busy the last year. I don't listen to much music these days. Anyway"—she pulled on the gloves— "guess I better go check on what our little crooner is up to."

"Whatever it is, you gotta get him up and about, to do the concert. A lot of soldiers are going to be disappointed if you don't."

"Ha. I'll do my best. Try not to salivate in any open wounds. I don't do messy."

The nurse laughed. "Promise."

Major Palmer strolled into the surgical area where she heard someone singing and playing an acoustical guitar. Immediately, she spotted a man sitting shirtless on an examining table as if he didn't have a care in the world. His olive skin and five-o'clock shadow slowed her steps to take in the entire picture. A well-toned physique surprised her, since she'd imagined a man with a beer gut and some missing teeth who possessed a nice voice. That wrong assumption gave her pause.

When he shifted his attention toward her and exhibited a smile on a wide mouth, Major Palmer decided she didn't much care for him. He owned the room and was apparently accustomed to being the center of attention. He stopped singing and cocked his head as he examined her from head to toe with what appeared to be appreciation. Now, the major was positive she didn't like him. For all she knew, Kade Atwood was another man who thought her looks meant she either wasn't very smart or could be treated as less than an equal.

"You must be the doctor," he said in a Southern drawl.

"Get that guitar out of here," she ordered.

An orderly grabbed the instrument out of his hands and disappeared.

"Now, wait a minute…" he complained as he surveyed the room, confused at the sudden change of atmosphere. "Be careful. That's important to me."

"I'm Major Palmer." She studied a tablet held up for her to read. "Says here you cut yourself on stage equipment when it was unloaded last night."

He twisted a bit to show her an open wound on his side. "A piece of wood splintered off and stabbed me." He flinched when she touched the area. "Major?"

She stepped back and stared at him, surprised at her sudden interest in the way his wavy brown hair fell down over his ears and how deep his voice sounded when he spoke slowly. Although not a particularly handsome man, there was definitely no denying his charisma. The interest in who he was, shocked her. How many men's romantic interest had she snubbed, outwitted, and rejected over the last couple of years? Her work always came first.

"What is it, Mr. Atwood?"

"Do all Army doctors look like you?" The beguiling smile and the flirtatious tone managed to irritate her further.

"Do all country music singers ask dumb questions?" she retorted.

He laughed then grabbed his side, groaning. "You're a real live wire, Major."

She put her stethoscope on his chest, causing him to cringe. "Be still."

"It's cold. Kinda like you," he said through clenched teeth.

Her nurse returned and held up the tablet again displaying X-rays.

"You've got a few pretty large fragments in here. I can remove what's causing you pain before infection sets in. I'll stitch you up here or, if you prefer, have one of our overworked pilots take you back to Frankfort, Germany where they're used to pampering our special guests here at Camp Shoot-First-Or-Die-Later. Either way, you'll require a tetanus shot. What's it going to be?"

He cringed and grabbed his side again then fell sideways on the examining table. An orderly helped him roll to his back. Blood oozed out as he tried to touch it. The major caught his hand and gave instructions for two attendants to sterilize the area.

"I'm guessing you're doing it here. Just be quick about it. I've got a concert to give."

"Prep him for a quick surgical procedure. Shouldn't be too big a deal, but we don't want pretty boy to miss his concert." She removed her gloves when he tried to sit up only to be pushed back down by the attendant.

"Hey, where you going? Aren't you going to take care of this?"

"I have to remove shrapnel from a leg next-door." This time, she glared at him from head to toe in the most obstinate way she could muster. "You are lower on my food chain list, whoever you are in Nashville. You'll live. The guy next door might lose a leg. I'll be here when I get here. The nurse can give you something for pain so you'll be ready when I get back." She glanced at the nurse. "Let me know when he stops complaining."

"Major Palmer?" Kade Atwood turned his head toward her and made a poor effort at a lopsided grin. "I appreciate this. If more soldiers need you, I can wait as long as it takes. I mean it. I'll be fine." His words were brave, but he'd turned pale.

"They're always my first priority, Mr. Atwood. Thank you for your permission." She turned and left.

~ ~ ~ ~

"She always so friendly?" Kade asked as one of the orderlies helped him finish undressing before hooking him up to tubes and wires.

"Only if you're a civilian. She doesn't appreciate non-military poking around, making suggestions as to how to run a war with no skin in the game. She works hard and has saved a lot of lives here. We all think she walks on water, if you get my drift."

"I'm a goodwill ambassador, not a politician."

"Lucky for you." He smiled, attaching tape to his chest. "Believe me, she wouldn't have been nearly as friendly."

"Bet I can win her over."

"I'll take that bet. Tough cookie."

"I specialize in tough cookies." He tried to laugh, when a pain shot through him so fast he drew up his legs. The last thing he heard when the orderly called to the nurse, "Better let the major know Mr. Country Music just passed out."

~ ~ ~ ~

"He's coming to, Major Palmer," the orderly said, checking the singer's pulse. "He's been sleeping like a baby. I didn't think he'd ever wake up."

Major Palmer checked his chart before examining the wound she'd stitched up. "Mr. Atwood, you—"

"Call me Kade."

"Okay, Kade. You had several wood fragments in your wound and had nicked a couple of blood vessels. I had to repair those besides cleaning out the mess you made. Your band is concerned you'll not be able to perform the concert tomorrow. I don't believe it's a problem, but—"

"I'm doing the concert." He fumbled at the dressing when the orderly smacked his hand.

Major Palmer looked over the top of the tablet at him. "You'll be a little sore, but as long as you don't do an Elvis jiggle, it should be okay. No heavy lifting for a few days. Give it a chance to heal. Don't want to rip it open. Overall, you're a pretty healthy guy."

"You're coming to the concert, aren't you?" he asked in a nonchalant tone. Instead of replying, she cranked his bed up to a sitting position. "Well?"

She shrugged. "I'm sorry, Mr.—I mean, Kade, I don't know any of your music. I'm more of a Mozart kind of listener."

"Put the ball, put the ball, on the golf tee. Let it roll, let it roll, let it roll." He smiled.

"What?" She felt her forehead pinch in confusion.

"Mozart's *Symphony No. 40 in G Minor*. If you can sing words to the classics, it's probably from the romance era." He began singing the words he'd just spoken to the tune of the 40th symphony.

"Well, what do you know?" she chuckled. "I didn't realize that."

"My mother was a music teacher, and my dad managed a small opera house. Since we were Southerners, it was a must I also learn the country music classics of Hank Snow, Lester Flatt and Earl Scruggs, Johnny Cash, and Willie Nelson, of course."

"Them, I know," she said in a cool tone. "You, I don't."

"You will after my concert."

"Guess I'd better try to attend. Hopefully, no one will require stitches or surgery for a few hours."

"How's the kid with the shrapnel? Did he lose his leg?"

"No. But he has a long road ahead of him. He's not out of the woods yet. We're sending him home for better care as soon as he's stable. He won't be able to make your concert." She walked toward the door. "Get some rest. I'll make rounds later tonight to see how you're doing."

"You don't have to do that just for me. I promise I'll follow orders like a good soldier."

She smiled in spite of herself. "Get over yourself. I do it for all my patients. And a good soldier wouldn't have gotten hurt from a few pieces of equipment falling on him."

"Man, you won't give me a break, will you?"

"Rest, Mr. Atwood. I mean, Kade." She wanted to smack the smug expression off his face when he gave her a military salute.

~ ~ ~ ~

Major Vivian Palmer wiped the fog from her bathroom mirror and examined herself with a critical eye. All the young men and women she hadn't been able to save and the ones she had were pieced together to survive, weighed heavy on her heart. Survive what? A life full of nightmares and PTSD? Was that what she was experiencing? Could it be time to go home?

Maybe loneliness had gotten the best of her. How long had it been since she'd share any kind of intimacy?

A touch? A kiss? Too long.

She began singing the words Kade taught her to one of her favorite Mozart symphonies. "Put the ball, put the ball, on the golf tee. Let it roll, let it roll, let it roll."

Strangely enough, it made her smile at her reflection in the mirror. The expression made her appear younger. Was it time for a break?

CHAPTER 2

L ate night tended to be the time-of-day Vivian enjoyed most. Except for the guards, many in the camp were asleep. She would slip out of her tent and do one more round to check on patients. At least, tonight, there were only two. The young man with the wounded leg and the country music star. Even before she entered the Mobile Army Surgical Hospital, she heard music. Inside, the music grew louder, drawing her to Kade Atwood's earlier location. The bed was empty.

She followed the music and found him sitting at the young soldier's bedside, playing his guitar and singing. The soldier had one hand behind his head that was propped up on extra pillows. He sang along with Kade. The two appeared to be oblivious of her presence. In that moment, she understood how the star's music could help to heal these men and women on the front lines of danger and national security.

Standing in the shadows, Vivian listened to the next two songs. Between them, the two men discussed home, and the soldier's fiancée. Kade pulled out his phone and showed him pictures of his labrador, a trained tracker. When he began a love song, Vivian stepped out into the open. The music stopped and the soldier stared at her with wide eyes. Kade cleared his throat and the soldier tried to straighten to a more sitting position.

"Major," the soldier said, as formally as if standing at attention.

"I guess you wrote that love song for a special lady back home?" she quizzed.

"I did. It's for my dog."

This time, Major Palmer couldn't resist a smile. "Corporal. Why aren't you asleep?" she asked, lifting his chart to scan quickly. His blood pressure and pulse had stabilized. She'd always heard that singing helped the soul. Perhaps it affected the soldier's vitals as well. A few hours ago, they had given her concern.

"Afraid that's my fault, Major Palmer," Kade admitted mischievously. "I figured since he wasn't going to get to come to the concert, I'd bring the concert to him. Sorry if I disturbed anyone. Hard to pass up a captive audience."

"Other than giving my nurses a case of heart flutters, no harm done."

"What makes your heart flutter, Major Palmer?"

"Drinking a glass of sweet tea while sitting on the front porch overlooking a creek where I used to go skinny-dipping." She chuckled at the soldier's blush. "Sorry, Corporal. I didn't mean to embarrass you. It appears Mr. Atwood's music took me back home too."

"Glad I could help," Kade confessed. "And where is home?"

"It's time for you two to go to bed. Corporal, you're due for pain meds in an hour. Better catch a nap before the nurse comes in and starts poking at you."

"Yes, ma'am. Thank you."

Turning her attention to the country music star, who now eyed her as if she might be on the menu, she pointed to the exit for him to return to his private area. "Out of here," she ordered. He limped past her. She followed him while carrying an LED lantern.

"I noticed you haven't eaten your dinner," she said, swinging the portable table away from the bed so he could get in easier. "You should eat. Singers burn up a lot of calories when they perform. Vitamins will help you heal."

"I got sidetracked."

"So, I noticed. It was nice of you to give the corporal a private concert. I guess you're not such a waste of time after all."

"I'm confused if I should be insulted or appreciative of your comment." He sat on the edge of his bed and placed the guitar beside him.

She didn't respond.

"When did you last eat, Major Palmer?"

"Actually, I believe it was breakfast. I've been busy most of the day, including surgery on you and the corporal. I'll go check if I can make us something hot."

"I'm pretty good in the kitchen. Let me help."

Vivian felt unsure of herself for the first time in years. Her heart raced at the sound of his voice and the recent memory of how his music affected her. Although not totally unpleasant, she willed her brain to resist his charms.

"I'll cook. But you can keep me company. The cook doesn't appreciate anyone messing around his equipment."

"But it's okay if you do?" he asked, scooting off the bed and grabbing his guitar.

"I outrank him." She pushed her shoulder-length ash-blonde hair behind her ears. "One of the perks of being in charge."

"And you strike me as a person who prefers being in charge."

"And you strike me as a man who likes to pry into other people's business."

"I'm always searching for the next big hit song. Maybe I'll write one about you when I leave." He leaned against the table where she created grilled cheese sandwiches. "You look amazing, by the way."

"Save your flirting for the nurses who have a hard time breathing when you're around."

"Don't you believe in romance, Major?"

"No. I believe in… Well, I'm not a romantic."

"Too bad. Bad marriage?"

"Never been married."

"Rotten boyfriend with a drug habit and a wife?"

"I'm not stupid, Mr. Atwood."

"It's Kade. Remember? I guess you've spent your time becoming a top-notch surgeon to prove to your family, yourself, or the women's lib crowd you didn't need help making it alone?"

Vivian pushed a plate of raw veggies and the hot grilled cheese sandwiches toward him. She walked to the refrigerator to retrieve an individual carton of milk. "Not that it's any of your business, but I became a surgeon because my father told me I could be anything I wanted to be, if I worked hard enough. He worked three jobs and saved for years so when I grew up, I could go to medical school. I didn't want my life to get tangled up in a relationship where a Romeo might feel threatened by my success or work ethic. If I had decided to be a dogcatcher, my family would have still been proud of me. My dad didn't live long enough to see me become a surgeon because a tractor fell on him and severed his leg. He bled out all alone. I swore then I'd give back for all his hard work so I could fulfill my dream. To be honest, I haven't had time to be touchy-feely for a jerk who only wanted me between the sheets." Vivian pushed herself up on a stool and tried to ignore him by pushing her food around.

"Aren't you going to eat?" Kade took a bite of the sandwich then pointed a carrot at her.

"I've lost my appetite."

"I'm sorry. I shouldn't have pried. Guess I'm used to getting my way when it comes to women."

"So I gathered."

"Can we start over?"

"Why? You'll sing tomorrow, go on to the next concert, either at another military camp or back home. We'll be a stamp on your passport. You are what you are. It's fine."

When they locked gazes, she figured he was trying to intimidate her, so she didn't break the gaze. The truth scared her a little because she liked him. Doing verbal combat kept him at a safe distance, in order to keep from acting like some of her foolish nurses.

"I think I like you, Major Palmer. Can we be friends and skip the lovers part? I could sure use someone like you in my life."

For whatever reason, his eyes always squinted when he smiled. It was rather endearing. "I'll see if my friend list has an opening." She grabbed a celery stick off his plate and chomped down on it. "No promises though."

"As your new friend," Kade said, pulling his plate away from her reach, "I want you to know I don't like people eating off my plate, even if they are prettier than a speckled pup. Get your own supper, Major."

Vivian choked on her laugh then started coughing until Kade slapped her on the back. "Did you just compare me to a dog?"

"I probably just saved your life, Major. I think you owe me now."

"Okay." She couldn't resist letting one corner of her mouth lift in amusement. "I suppose I'll have to acquiesce to your proposal. We can be friends. I might enjoy a little comic relief from time to time. Can you fill that particular gap in my life?"

"I'm a pretty funny guy. I'm guessing you don't enjoy country music, but I'm going to ask you to start listening to my music. You know, so you'll see what a great guy I am."

"I'm going to need you to read the handbook on field dressing a gunshot wound, so you'll understand I'm a no-nonsense kind of girl."

"Does it involve duct tape and superglue? Shoot. Child's play."

Once more, Vivian laughed out loud.

"See? I'm hilarious."

"You mean ridiculous." She patted him on the forearm, drawing his attention downward then back up to her face, which he searched long and hard. Slowly, she withdrew her hand and eased off the stool. "Finish up. I need to get you back in bed."

He smirked. "Just friends, Major. No hanky-panky."

Normally, she would have bombarded a man with enough insults his head would be spinning. But for whatever reason, Kade made it sound funny. "No worries there, Slick. You're not even close to my type."

"What is your type? I'll be on the lookout for one of those. What are friends for, right?"

"No, thanks. I'm pretty sure he doesn't exist. Besides, I may be going home soon and, if history repeats itself, like it does with most soldiers, I'll require therapy or some kind of dangerous hobby to keep my head on straight."

"Remember, I'm a phone call away. I'll give you the info before I leave."

"Oh. You were serious about the friend thing." She couldn't help but burst out laughing again when he frowned.

A male nurse joined them in the kitchen. "Major Palmer, I took care of the corporal. Is there anything else?"

"Yes. When Mr. Atwood finishes his supper, could you escort him back to his quarters for me? I'm on call early tomorrow."

"Yes, ma'am. Happy to."

"Thank you, Sergeant." She walked past Kade and saluted him like he had her earlier in the day. "Good night, Slick. I'll try and make the concert."

~ ~ ~ ~

As the major walked away, Kade wished instantly he could have stopped her. Any other time, he would have charmed the claws off a grizzly bear. Why not this time? Why did he become tongue-tied, as if experiencing his first crush in high school?

Over the years, he'd become accustomed to getting

what he wanted at the drop of a hat. Women were always more than willing to be his arm candy, although he'd resisted most of those. The fan base who followed him were amazing, and he appreciated each and every one of them. The truth was, though, he wanted to keep most of them at a distance when offstage.

Another country music star who made it big early in life had shared his wisdom and experience when Kade first hit the big time.

"I can see your talent is going to make you a huge star. Never lose sight of who you are or where you came from. The bright lights, opportunities, and adoration of fans can blind you of the path you intended to take. It will rob you of your joy and, most of all, your music."

He'd taken the advice to heart even though, at times, he fell for a pretty face. Disappointment followed, when he discovered it was the fame, fortune, and bright lights she loved. Walking away had never felt like a missed opportunity until tonight when Major Palmer left him in the care of a kid who couldn't be that long out of high school. She didn't care about his celebrity status, or if he had more money than she would ever see, especially if this military life was going to be her career.

On the way back to bed, he decided to engage the male nurse. "What's Major Palmer's story? Married? Divorced? Lover?" He couldn't help but notice the shy grin on the face of his escort.

"Major Palmer is well respected here. She's saved a lot of lives and shares the success with all of us. Rarely takes time off unless the higher-ups insist on it. Several of the officers have become friends with her, but no romance as far as I know. She is a looker. I'll give ya that. Wouldn't mind getting on her good side, but she is way out of my league. Her backstory is a mystery to us. She doesn't talk personal stuff. Besides, we don't have a lot of time for that here. It's pretty much life or death here and, when it isn't, then we try sleep."

"A rough life. I appreciate what you do."

"Thanks. The troops will appreciate you being here for a little walk down memory lane. Take their minds off the other world they live in."

"Glad I came." He sat down on his bed after propping his guitar against the nightstand. "Until tomorrow, Corporal."

He gave a thumbs-up and left Kade there in the near dark. A small LED shone a ribbon of light from the other room. However long it took, he wanted to be more than just a friend—if Major Palmer let him in. He'd navigated difficult roads before. What was one more? Closing his eyes, the lyrics to a forming song carried him into sleep. For the first time in months, he slept soundly, dreaming of a woman who made a difference each day without any monetary reward or notoriety. It had been a while since he'd met a genuinely caring person who used their talents to make the world a better place.

CHAPTER 3

"Incoming bird," a voice announced over the speaker. "Wounded on board. Prisoners on second bird. Third helo on way. Took fire."

"What's going on?" Kade grabbed the sleeve of a medic who headed out of the surgery center.

"Wounded. Best stay out of the way, sir." The medic disappeared.

Kade made it to the exit and observed the organized chaos going on in the camp. There were a number of military rushing across open ground between tents when he spotted Dr. Palmer. She wore a helmet with the chin straps dangling down her jawline. Somehow, she'd managed to take the ordinary and turn it into a fashion statement. Her crisp, clean fatigues were in sharp contrast to such a dusty place. The smell of latrines and smoke from burning trash; he could only guess what else might be in burn pits. She climbed into a Hummer void of doors that bore a white cross on the hood. The rest of the Hummers wore the same insignia.

When she spotted him, her chin went up as if in a

greeting, then he noticed her frowning. A second later, he realized he probably didn't matter in the anticipation of friends lost, dying, and wounded. She bore a kind of hard-core tenaciousness he'd hadn't witnessed in a woman in a long time.

A general ran up to the Hummer and leaned in to say a few words to her then placed a hand on her shoulder. Whatever he said to her, she nodded, followed by a wide smile. She waved him off, causing him to take a step back. The Hummer followed two other ambulance vehicles at the same time the general pivoted and stared straight at him. The general exhibited a tight jaw and a sour face. Kade imagined the man didn't hold much respect for anyone outside the military.

His unwavering glare created the impression they had entered a pissing contest. The general approached in a slow and easy gait, reminding him of the actor George C. Scott from the General Patton movie. Even from where he stood, Kade detected the man's powerful influence as if it were a loaded gun.

"How are you feeling, son?" The deep voice reaffirmed Kade's first impression of a tough-as-nails kind of man.

"Much better, sir." Kade couldn't help but drop his arms to his side and demonstrate a kind of at-attention stance.

"Glad to hear it." The general glanced back over his shoulder and watched the vehicles disappear in a dust cloud so typical in this dry part of Afghanistan. Slowly, he turned back and eyeballed the country singer. "Heard Major Palmer stitched you up."

"Yes, sir. Damn good doctor."

"I also heard you gave a private concert to a man who

ships out today for better medical care. Thanks for taking the time."

"My honor, sir. The least I can do."

"Bad news is the Taliban are on the move in this direction. We're canceling your concert. I can put you and your band on the medivac plane with what appears to be more seriously wounded men coming in now. Not sure if Vivian and her team can do it all here."

"Vivian?"

"Major Palmer. Sorry." He cocked his head, squinting as if the sun blinded him. "She's a good friend and pretty special to all of us. Especially me."

"I see."

The general slapped him on the arm, which felt like a precursor to a next time when it might be harder.

"Good. She doesn't need any distractions during these next few hours."

"If it's all the same to you, I think I'll stay. Maybe I can spread a little good cheer."

"Listen, son, I know you mean well, but a few songs aren't going to fix the wrongs here. And we don't have time to babysit a bunch of honky-tonk Romeos."

"Wow." Kade raised his chin, determined to resist the attempt at intimidation. "How about this? I put my band on the plane, and I stick around to visit the men and women. Maybe a few songs at dinner or whenever you say is a good time. I don't need a band for that. Got my guitar and happy to assist in any way I can—sir."

"Have your people ready to leave by 1700 hours. I'll let you know if I decide you can stay behind. But don't count on it. I'll have someone move your things back to the guest quarters."

"All I have is my guitar."

"A warning: Stay out of the way when the medical teams return. They will run over you and never look back. Those soldiers are their priority."

"Will do."

Kade found his guitar and changed into his clothes folded at the foot of his bed. Activity in the surgical wing now reminded him of a beehive where everyone had a job and nothing would stop them from completing their assigned task.

People sidestepped him while shouting orders or asking for assistance as the wounded began arriving. There were moments he thought he'd become invisible, as shouts of despair, crying, and encouragement flooded the spaces. The hustle of soldiers, medical personnel, and wounded was organized chaos that both confused and inspired him.

"Kade Atwood." A man grinned from his gurney. "Are you goin' to sing to us in here?"

"You bet, soldier. What's your name?"

"Private Timothy Stevens, sir."

"Private, I'm Major Palmer." She pushed in front of Kade and checked the soldier's pulse. "You took a hard hit, soldier. I'm going to operate on you ASAP. Then I'm putting you on the medivac plane. How's that sound?"

"It sounds…" He closed his eyes and began to shake.

"Get this soldier ready and…"

Kade stared at the soldier, who appeared to be pumping out blood at an alarming rate. Major Palmer put her hand down on the wound to control the flow as assistants swarmed around him and carried the gurney away. In seconds, she had disappeared. Kade took a deep breath and realized he now knew how it must feel to be hit by a ton of bricks.

"I'm here to take you to your quarters, Mr. Atwood." A young private with a black eye and a reddish scar down his jaw approached him. "Do you have anything I should carry for you? Orders are you were to take it easy a day or so."

"No thanks, Private. Let's go."

~ ~ ~ ~

"Hell of a day, Vivian," commented General Morgan when he signed off on sending two soldiers on to Germany for care they couldn't provide. "You and your team did everything right and made miracles happen."

"Thanks, sir."

"Hey, it's just us. It's okay to use my name."

"I appreciate you sticking around and encouraging us. It means a lot."

"I'll be back to speak to each soldier tomorrow, when they are up for it. Let me know when it's a good time. I'm headed out to see the others off. I'll probably stay out at Bagram Airfield tonight to make sure things run smoothly. When I know they've left Afghan airspace, I'll relax. Since it will be late, I don't want to put any more people in danger. We'll head back in the morning."

"And the prisoners?"

"Secured. Nothing life-threatening. They'll be checked over tomorrow. They'll head to interrogation if our resident spooks are on board with the transfer."

"Be careful, Bud. Thanks for your help today. I know the troops are disappointed the concert had to be canceled. Is the Atwood band already at the airport?"

"All except the big country music star. Kade Atwood wouldn't take no for an answer. Sent me a note saying he'd donate the proceeds from his next concert to whatever military charity we wanted, if he could stay and cheer these people on."

"What? That's a lot of money. I have to admit, the guy does have a way with these men and women. I saw it yesterday."

"Just between me and you"—he winked— "I think he may want to stay for another reason. It doesn't have anything to do with soldier morale." He patted her arm. "And you're blushing. Watch yourself. These good ole boys from back home come and go, never knowing the hell waiting in the trenches. He's no different. Probably wanting inspiration for a hit song and a story to tell. These guys have a trail of broken hearts, never understanding how it affects the real heroes of his songs."

"No worries, Bud. I'm not looking for romance."

"Maybe not. But I have a feeling it might be looking for you."

~ ~ ~ ~

Major Vivian Palmer rubbed her sore eyes then sighed with exhaustion after caring for the wounded. Thankfully, most had surface wounds that would heal soon enough. The PTSD remained a bigger concern, in her opinion, especially when these soldiers returned home. As long as they were here, the distraction of a war zone kept the adrenalin bubbling like a smoking volcano that could blow any time. This applied to her as well.

The others had wait-and-see wounds that hopefully wouldn't require surgery. Several others, she and the other doctors managed to stabilize enough to send on to

Germany. Even with all the undivided attention they tried to give each of the wounded, one died, and two other injured soldiers, required her surgery magic and would live to fight another day. She decided to observe them a couple of days then ascertain whether to send them home for rehabilitation or back to their units. Time away from this place would be the best medicine, and they deserved it. Hopefully, they could finish their service time in the States.

A hot shower turned out to be lukewarm. At least, removing grime and blood worked wonders. A clean pair of fatigues meant she'd worn them twice and had saved them for a time when she could bathe. Pulling on a camouflage T-shirt she'd washed in a sink the day before, she noticed how it hugged her body as she stood before a mirror that had cracks and spider veins throughout. The reflection appeared refreshed instead of overworked. The discarded attire, blood speckled and grimy, went into a laundry bag. Thankfully, her name was well established on the labels and would be returned in the near future. Not that she cared. It didn't matter since she had no place to go.

The image of Kade Atwood entered her brain, remembering him singing to the soldier the night before. Did she spot him walking around the camp? A man standing in the door of the surgery tent had watched her when she went out to the helicopters bringing in the wounded. Surely, he wasn't wandering around yet. Idiot should have left with his band.

Thunderous applause reached her from the mess tent, across from their makeshift hospital. She pulled her hair up into a ponytail while she made a security check up and down the row of structures used as barracks for the soldiers and other staff.

"Hey," she called to a soldier with an MP insignia on his sleeve. "What's going on? I thought I heard applause and yelling."

"Yes, ma'am. Kade Atwood is singing while the men eat their dinner. It's just him and his guitar. I haven't seen that many smiles or heard so much laughter since I got over here. The guy can tell a story."

"Who's watching the store, then?" she asked. Security might be compromised.

"Everyone is on rotation as usual. Kade said he'd stick around and sing for each shift and for those in the medical unit if he got permission. I should get going, Major Palmer."

"Thanks. Go ahead."

He stepped away then backed up and took a piece of paper out of his shirt pocket. "Sorry, Major. Nearly forgot. He said to give you this."

She nodded as she accepted the note. Taking a deep breath, she worried the singer might be getting to the sensible side of her. "This isn't going to happen," she mumbled. Temptation got the better of her. Opening the folded paper she read the simple words, *Thanks for all you do. You're my hero.* She tucked the paper in her pants pocket. Maybe she'd read it again later.

Lowering her chin, she proceeded with a determined yet irritated speed to her step. Pausing outside the mess hall, she stole a glance through the double doors to see the country music sensation sitting up front on a barstool singing his heart out to the dinner crowd. It both frustrated and softened her turbulent emotions, knowing he could have chosen to be someplace safe and clean instead of this hellhole. Although her stomach growled with hunger, she decided to make rounds as a distraction. She encouraged two nurses to go get dinner and enjoy the show. They started to hug her then straightened when she leveled a don't-make-me-change-my-mind warning glare.

She spent the first hour checking the patients and talking to them if they were awake. The following hour and a half were filled with paperwork. She wrote a quick letter to the families of the wounded to say their loved one was being cared for and she'd do her best to send them home soon. The idea people waited for them to return home gave her clarity as to why she had to continue this job as long as she could make a difference.

"I hoped you'd come to dinner tonight," came a deep voice from the entrance to the medical unit.

She stood and approached Kade Atwood. "Are you all right? Let me check your wound. You probably overdid it. Sit down over here."

He did as she asked and climbed up on an examining table. "Never did I ever imagine I'd be glad I was injured so I'd get a little attention." Kade leaned forward and smiled mischievously.

"Better enjoy it. I doubt the healthcare system back home will give you such a first-class medical facility to cover your ego." Raising his shirt, she touched around the wound.

He flinched.

"Cold hands, or did that hurt?" She forced mock contempt.

"I'm not sure if it was your tone or my ego. Either way, it's bruised. I'm probably hemorrhaging on the inside. I'm hurt."

She jerked his shirt down and tilted her head to stare

at his smiling mouth. It took a lot of willpower to expel a disgusted sigh as she shoved her hands into her pants pockets. "I guess you're here to sing for my patients. I'm sure they'll enjoy it." She waved a corporal over to assist. "Could you escort Mr. Atwood around the medical quarters for his performance? Make sure he has something to sit on. I don't want him straining those stitches."

"Aren't you going to stay?" He slid off the table and stood a breath away from her.

She tilted her head and locked onto his amused eyes that twinkled with mischief. "I think I'll go get supper. It's been a long day."

CHAPTER 4

The following day, Kade continued entertaining patients, nurses, soldiers, and whoever would listen to him sing. It did not go unnoticed by Vivian how the country music star visited each patient for as long as they needed. The staff shared how he wrote letters home for them if they were too weak or injured. Her heart melted a little when she watched him relieve one of the staff to feed a patient. He laughed at the corny jokes of the soldiers and swapped stories of his own upbringing. Not once did he brag on his fame or how important the world treated him back home.

"Are you trying for the Mother Teresa award?" Vivian asked as she read over a chart before checking the pale soldier's vitals. "You're going to spoil these people and, when you leave, I'm going to have to sing for them."

"Sing for me now. I can always use another backup singer." Kade propped his arms on the guitar he balanced in his lap.

"Sorry to tell you this, but I couldn't carry a tune in a bucket. I can cut you open and sew you up, however."

"Everyone has a gift. You save lives," he reminded her.

"I'm starting to believe maybe you do, too, hotshot. Thanks for sticking around. I haven't seen this kind of morale in quite a while. Guess you're not just a pretty face after all." She handed the chart off to a nurse and jammed her hands in the pockets of her lab coat. "Can I buy you dinner tonight? My treat." She laughed softly.

Another medical personnel, Dr. Wilkins, tapped Kade on the shoulder. "Better take her up on it. She's kind of stingy with her money. Oh wait. Meals are one of the perks of the job." He frowned and shook his head. "Better pass on it. It's not that great."

"Yeah, but the company would be tolerable, right?" Kade said seriously.

Dr. Wilkins shrugged. "It's okay, I guess. She is easy on the eyes. Hey, how come you never asked me out on a date?" he asked Vivian indignantly.

She pushed him aside to walk away. "For one thing, this isn't a date." She raised her chin and stared down her nose at Kade to make sure he understood the message before speaking to Dr. Wilkins again. "Reason number two is you're married and the father of five kids. Some doctor you are, if you don't know how that happened." She pointed to Dr. Wilkins then to Kade. "Don't let him operate on you. I'll see you tonight. Dress casual. It's not a fancy place." Before he could respond, she exited the room.

"Did I just get lucky?" Kade asked, beaming a lopsided grin. Several patients cheered for him.

General Morgan walked up behind him and slapped him on the back as he passed. "I wouldn't count on that, son. Don't misunderstand her gesture."

"I'm pretty charming," Kade said confidently.

Both the doctor and the general met each other's skeptical expression then laughed long and hard.

~ ~ ~ ~

Kade anticipated a drab evening draped in camouflage and dim light for his first date with Vivian, as he'd begun to call her in his mind. Was the dinner a peace offering between them? It wasn't lost on him how she appeared to appreciate his singing and efforts to bring a little comfort to this terrible place so far from home. He'd particularly enjoyed the half grin on those lips. He couldn't stop imagining if they might be firm and soft at the same time. Tonight, might be his last chance to make a better impression than he had at the beginning. Enlisting help from her grateful fan club was the easy part.

"What are you doing here?" Vivian asked when Kade showed up at her tent. She eyed him from head to toe. "I see you wore your good clothes."

"Yep. Since this is our first date—"

"This isn't a date," she reminded him, smirking as she shifted her weight to one hip. "It's a thank-you for time served." She pointed to his outfit of cowboy boots and Western-style shirt. "Pretty sharp out here in the middle of nowhere." Her attention went to the black cowboy hat. "This I like."

"I hoped you would, ma'am." Kade laid a hand on his heart. "I reckon I'm plum tickled to hear you say those kind words."

Vivian laughed and shooed him out the door. "Let's

go before you start talking like John Wayne. If you call anyone 'pilgrim' tonight, I'm leaving you at the table all alone."

He offered his arm and felt a quiet kind of pleasure when she slipped her hand through the opening.

Vivian had applied a little lip gloss and mascara, softening her usual stern expression. He caught a whiff of what smelled like soap, and her hair fell down around her shoulders. Even her clothes were more civilian than military.

"You're lookin' pretty good yourself there, Major. May I call you Vivian, since this is our first non-date?"

"Sure. But don't let it go to your head. I'm just a friend, not a starstruck groupie who faints when you sing."

"Noted. With friends like you, I need all the groupies I can get though. You aren't helping my ego much."

"I'm happy to keep your ego in check so you'll stay humble."

"You're doing a great job, Vivian. You've had me second-guessing myself since I laid eyes on you."

This caused her to laugh out loud. He could have sworn for a second, she hugged his arm and leaned in a bit closer. The idea that it mattered to him if she was impressed by his efforts, surprised him.

"Thanks for the note, but I'm not a hero."

"I'll be the judge of that." Did his heart lurch when she smiled up at him?

They arrived at what had been the mess hall. A sign posted outside said The Whiskey and Sweet Tea Café. Someone had rescued the tiny solar Christmas lights and attached them around the door, which was opened by a soldier who ushered them inside. A makeshift podium where Dr. Wilkins stared down at a blank notebook blocked their way. He glanced up.

"Can I help you?" His voice sounded stuffy and no nonsense.

"Come on," Vivian sighed. "What is this?"

"I have a reservation for two," Kade said calmly. "For Kade Atwood."

"Well, why didn't you say so? Nice to have you." The doctor snapped his fingers, and a corporal scurried out with a folded towel over his arm. "Take Mr. Atwood and his guest to the VIP room. Enjoy your meal."

Vivian chuckled when Kade took her hand in his. For a second, he feared she would pull away from what she might consider an intimate move this soon in their relationship. She did not resist as he followed the corporal, pretend waiter, to the VIP room. The truth remained, it was a corner of the mess hall that had been petitioned off with a piece of canvas and bedsheets. More twinkle lights and a couple of LED lanterns placed to give the area an added romantic vibe. A flickering candle placed in a jar adorned the table.

Kade pulled a chair out for her and then seated himself across the table. A second pretend waiter appeared carrying striped menus made from cardboard with a piece of Christmas ribbon attached to the top. The menu consisted of a list of four things.

The waiter pointed to an item. "Tonight, we have a special on vintage sweet tea, with several ice cubes. As you know, that is a rarity here. I recommend a glass, ma'am. Would you like to try that?"

"Yes, please."

"Make that two," Kade added, focusing on the amused expression Vivian now wore as she turned her complete attention to him.

"I see you have gone to a lot of trouble," she said as the waiter slipped away. She switched to a Southern accent. "And for little ole me?"

Kade enjoyed this new side of her, the playful, normal human being side. "I had plenty of help. You're kind of a rock star around here. People wanted to be part of making a nice evening for you."

"I was supposed to be taking you to dinner. Not the other way around. I'm sincerely touched." Vivian's voice turned soft as she reached across the table and gently touched his hand for a second. But it was long enough for him to grab it and hold as the sweet tea arrived in disposable cups.

"Here's to new friendships," he said, lifting his cup but continuing to hold her hand.

She managed to slip free in spite of his grasp and raised her own cup. "To new friendships. May they last beyond tomorrow."

They pretended to explore the menu choices for something special in spite of there being a total of one entrée and two sides. Small talk followed consisting of little details about their lives outside the war zone.

"Is that music I hear?" Vivian asked as she tilted her head.

"I couldn't find any classical we could dance to, so I downloaded a few old Kenny G tunes. I hoped they would be a good substitute."

"I'm glad you didn't decide on country, considering I don't know any Texas two-step moves. Matter of fact, I'm not sure I know any dance moves."

He pushed his chair back and went to her side to offer a hand. "Perfect. Then we can do the old-fashioned slow two-step. I don't feel like jumping around anyway. The thought of more stitches isn't my cup of tea. No pun intended."

Vivian took his hand and let him guide her to a small open space. A wave of shyness came over him as he slipped his arm around her waist until she stepped closer and leveled a beguiling smile at him.

"I'm having a really good time, Kade. Thank you. This is much better than what I had planned. Guess I'm still in your debt." They moved back and forth to the slow tunes.

"That's what I'm counting on. You're kind of my favorite doctor now. Good to have friends in high places in case you trip over your feet and stab yourself with music equipment. Maybe after you're home, you can go on the road as my personal physician to make sure I don't injure myself again."

"Sorry. I can't fix clumsy. My skills will be required elsewhere. Maybe I can prescribe you something as part of the therapy or healing process. However, if word got out about that little perk, I'd continue to be an overworked doctor."

"Whatever, as long as I can see you again." He might be rushing things, but in Afghanistan, it felt like this was how things worked if you wanted to survive.

Vivian slipped her hand up his arm and around his neck and laid her cheek against his. "You have gone to a lot of trouble. Chances are we only have now. Let's not talk options. Apparently, we both are in need of a friend who has nothing to do with reality. I don't expect anything from you, Kade Atwood. Don't make promises to me because you're grateful or caught up in the moment. Being friends is a gift people like us don't always get."

"Maybe so." He pulled her tighter against his chest and, for the first time in a long time, he experienced peace at being whole. Living in the bright lights of stardom had dimmed his focus on the real world. Emptiness crowded into his world with fake admiration, money, material things, and nonstop travel. All he really wanted was to put down roots. Vivian made him envision the possible so clearly now.

"Major, Mr. Atwood," It was one of Afghan medical staff. "We need to clean up and put things back for the morning schedule." Their waiter had returned to being serious.

"Of course. Thank you, Rasheed. I'll walk Major Palmer home then come back to help."

"No, sir. We got this." His face creased into a frown. "My pleasure. Take as long as you want."

Kade stepped aside for Vivian to walk in front of him. He glanced back at the soldiers and Afghan and mouthed "thank you." They gave a thumbs-up in return.

Vivians's tent was closer than it seemed earlier, making Kade slow his steps to prolong the evening. The wind had picked up, causing tent flaps and barracks' roofs to snap in harmony. The sliver of moon came and went behind rolling clouds and dust. Once more, he slipped Vivian's arm through his, hoping this wouldn't be the last time they spent together.

"Well, this is where I live. I'd invite you in, but I have early rounds in the morning, unless I get a call sooner. Beauty rest is a must in this place." Vivian had started to open the door when Kade slipped his arm around her waist and pulled her to his chest. He wondered if she sensed his hesitation or felt the hammering of his heart.

She leveled a longing gaze at him and wrapped her arms around his neck. "Kade," was all she said before he captured her mouth in a passionate kiss he would never forget. When she withdrew and stroked his face, he knew without a doubt he'd found the missing element in his life. Whatever would make this permanent, he planned to make it his top priority.

"I know it's too soon to be feeling this way, Vivian, so I'm just going to say good night." He took the hand on his cheek and kissed it. "It would be too easy to take advantage of you in a place like this. I want you to know I have good intentions, and I plan to show you I can be more than your friend. I'm willing to take it as slow as you want. But I'm letting you know right now that I—"

Movement inside her quarters caught his eye. He pushed her behind him.

She followed his line of sight. "What is it?" She started around him, but he cut her off. "That's strange. I left my LED lantern on. I never turn it off when I leave at night."

"You've got company. Let's back up and get a guard."

When they pivoted to leave, a dark shadow exited her tent and loomed in front of them. A quick club made contact with Kade's gut, knocking the wind out of him. Stumbling backward, he managed to reach for Vivian. With her eyes wide with terror, he realized they were under attack. Another blow hit him in the bend of his knees, sending him crashing to the ground. He struggled to stand on wobbly legs as the insurgent pushed Vivian inside her quarters.

CHAPTER 5

Vivian stumbled as the attacker shoved her inside her quarters. The sound of gunfire and loud voices shouting orders kept the strange man hunched before her turning to glance over his shoulder. Without warning, he focused his attention on her, shouting words she couldn't understand. He lunged at her, knocking her down on the bed. The smell of body odor mixed with bad breath nearly made her vomit. His hands became invasive as he tried to undo her clothing.

Survival mode kicked in, and she scratched, punched, and screamed as loud as she could to distract him from furthering the attack. It worked until he tried to capture her hands slapping at his ears and eyes. When her body was losing the battle against a much stronger man, he was lifted off her like a child's toy and tossed across the open space, crashing into the makeshift dresser. Kade reached down and jerked her up without taking his eyes off the insurgent struggling to his feet.

Kade ran at the intruder before he regained confidence and slugged him in the jaw several times, but the man came right back at him, swinging a knife he pulled from under his vest. One connected to Kade's side where he'd been injured, causing him to stagger back in pain.

Vivian pulled the weapon she carried, jumped in front of Kade, and opened fire into the Afghan. Even before he fell, eyes wide with surprise, Kade managed to relieve her of the gun. She spun around and fell into his one free arm, shaking.

"Do you have another weapon, Vivian?"

"No. This is what I carry while I'm in the compound. If I leave, I have an M16."

"Great. Where is it?" Kade went to the door and peeked out. "Looks like the camp has been overrun. Where is a safe place?"

"I'm going to the hospital. My patients need me. My M16 is kept there in case we have to protect the wounded in this kind of scenario."

"Let's go. I'm keeping this weapon. If the insurgents break through this far, I want you to make a beeline to the hospital. I'll hold them off until help comes. Got another magazine for this thing?"

Vivian slipped out of his protective embrace and retrieved two magazines from the drawer in the nightstand. "Got it. Let's go. Sounds like they're getting closer."

Gunfire caused them to hunker down as they ran toward the hospital. She spotted the cook carrying his weapon as he rushed forward to stand next to Kade. Two more soldiers, usually orderlies, waited at the entrance. Vivian rushed inside where Dr. Wilkins tossed her the M16 kept in a locked container.

"I was hoping you'd be back." He nodded at the

weapon. "It's ready to go. Sling it, and let's check on the patients. They're nervous. A couple offered to help. I didn't say no if I thought they could manage."

Vivian swung the M16 to her shoulder, aware of the weight.

"What is that from?" Dr. Wilkins asked as he pointed to the blood splatter on her neck and shirt. "Where's pretty boy?"

"I'll explain later. Let's get things secured. Where are the nurses?"

"All here except Rasheed. Still cleaning up after your romantic dinner. The others are positioned near patients. These nurses are a bunch of badasses."

Vivian couldn't help but grin at the remark as she continued into the ward where most of the patients tried to push themselves up in their beds. A few already sitting up showed their weapons then slipped them back under the covers. Others had roused enough to pull on trousers and stood bare-chested.

First thing, she checked their wounds to make sure no one was bleeding. Chances were good their blood pressure had spiked, considering the situation, but that was to be expected so she didn't check it.

Satisfied the patients were reasonably secure, she ordered a wounded sergeant to double-check weapons in case medication had impeded the preparation of readiness. "Yes, ma'am, Major. I already did that."

"You're a good man, Sergeant. Thank you."

Kade hurried inside and called out to her when she noticed blood soaking through his clothes.

"Let me have a look at that," she ordered.

"We don't have time. I'm fine. The Taliban is slowly making their way toward us."

Vivian twisted her body to survey the patients who closely watched her. "I guess we'd better get ready. Look nonthreatening, men, if they get this far. Hopefully, our guys will stop them."

Kade reached out and squeezed her arm quickly to offer support. At the same time, several soldiers exchanged glances as if he'd violated the rule not to touch the holy grail. No way this bunch would let the Taliban get in without a fight. The wounded were ready as were the nurses who now had transformed from angels of mercy to characters out of the *Call of Duty: Modern Warfare* video game. Gone were the smiles and flirting, replaced with steely-eyed glares he thought might melt iron.

The ache in his side burned and throbbed. He didn't want to complain considering everyone in the room had met the enemy and death up close and personal. They looked to Vivian for her complete calm and confidence, in spite of what she'd been through in the last hour. He was thankful he'd managed to rally and give the Afghan a taste of justice. When the Afghan pulled a knife and started to lunge at him, Vivian had stepped in and saved his life.

"Major! Major!" came a voice from the outer door.

"Dr. Wilkins, can you take over here?"

He nodded as she exited with Kade on her heels. "Careful, Vivian. We don't know—"

"I know who it is. Relax. I'm a soldier, not a baby," she said drily. "I know you're trying to help. I have to do my job."

Kade ignored her and pushed in front of her. Several soldiers were carrying in General Morgan, who was cussing and threatening loud enough to wake the dead. He appeared to be in bad shape, so Vivian pointed to the surgery section and yelled for a nurse. When they placed him on the examining table, Vivian leaned over him.

He calmed. "Patch me up, and I'll get out of your hair. Several of our boys were hurt."

"With all due respect, General Morgan, shut the hell up. I'm the boss in here. Not you."

"You're being insubordinate, Major," he said, letting out a deep sigh.

"Yes, sir, I am. Nonetheless, let me have a look. If you start whining like a little girl and pretending you want to get back in the action, I'm going to shoot some really good stuff in your butt to get a little peace and quiet so I can work. Do we understand each other?"

Kade was relieved when the angry expression on the man's face added a thin smile as he closed his eyes. "I don't like needles."

"I don't like big babies, so I guess we're even." She cut his shirt away carefully.

Kade joined the two soldiers guarding the front door while Vivian gave orders for the general's care.

"Boy, I wish I could get away with talking to an officer like that." The young soldier elbowed Kade then switched back to intense observation of the outside. The other soldier turned the light behind them out then went in and did the same where the wounded were waiting. He pulled the heavy piece of canvas, hanging on a rod, across the opening to close off the area.

"I think those T-men—"

"What?" Kade asked.

"Short for Taliban. Anyway, I think they're in retreat. They were scrambling back into the darkness like a bunch of rats," the first soldier said nonchalantly then gave a little nervous chuckle. "Gonna be hell to pay when we find out how they made it inside."

"Has this happened before?" Kade adjusted and checked his weapon.

"Nope. Never. They're getting a little braver, since they know we're all pulling out in a few months. I guess they want us to know things are about to go back to the way they were before we came. The women and the kids are the ones who are going to suffer."

The realization hit him that this was a world he'd never expected. How did they deal with the uncertainty? The most unnerving thing he'd ever experienced was when a love-crazed fan slipped past his security and wanted to have his baby. Now, it felt like he should apologize to these men and women in uniform.

Now, with all this new kind of chaos, he realized why Dr. Vivian Palmer didn't have time for romance. Every day was an epic experience in life and death. The thought he wanted to be there for her when this war ended, overwhelmed him. Now, he understood why PTSD and veteran suicide was such a problem after these warriors came home. If he made it home, things were going to change.

"Corporal, could you come help us lift the general into a bed since he's out cold? He's dead weight right now." Major Palmer appeared and tilted her head for the corporal to follow her.

"Yes, ma'am." He slung his weapon to his shoulder and moved toward her.

Kade jammed his weapon into the pocket of his jacket and was following the corporal when she held up her hand and frowned.

"Where do you think you're going? You're bleeding, and I'm going to look at the wound. I'll be back in a minute. Get in there and on the table." She pivoted and disappeared into the patient section of the hospital.

"Don't want to make her mad, Mr. Atwood, sir."

"It's Kade."

"Kade, if you aren't there when she gets back, she'll have one of us take care of it and, honestly"—he switched his attention from the outside to him—"I'm not in a very good mood. I would hate to accidently shoot you."

"Understood. Thanks."

The soldier raised his chin in acceptance of Kade's decision and refocused on the outside corridor that periodically flashed with gunfire. He couldn't decide if the soldier's words were a credible threat, but he thought the decision to obey definitely more prudent than to push his luck.

"There you are," Vivian said to him as the nurse came alongside and handed her a chart.

He guessed it had his name on it, since the nurse was giving him sideways glances and batting her eyelashes rapid-fire.

"Thanks, Molly. Can you clear the mess over there to the trash while I do this? Thanks. Oh, and make sure the general is prepped for surgery. I'm going in tonight."

The nurse gave a thumbs-up.

"Strip," she ordered when the nurse left the room.

"I thought we were keeping this casual," he joked. When she arched an eyebrow of contempt, he unbuttoned his shirt.

Vivian pulled his bandage away and cleaned the area. "You pulled a few stitches, and the whole area is dirty.

I'm going to shoot you with a heavy antibiotic so these nasty germs won't get you down. I'm not asking, by the way." Before he could protest, she jabbed the needle into a vial and extracted the medicine. "Okay, pretty boy, you're going to need to drop your pants."

This scenario had played out differently in his head when he thought about how the evening might end. When he didn't obey immediately, she held up the needle like Dr. Frankenstein and snickered.

"Maybe shoot that in my arm instead?" He eased off the table.

"How about I call in one of those big Marines to help you? That might be more fun for me, anyway. Afterward, I'm sure there will be comments concerning your lack of—"

"Fine," he snapped. He unzipped his pants and turned his back to her. A soft hand tugged his pants down on his hip, followed by a cool swab, smelling of alcohol. A jab of pain caused him to suck in his breath then straighten. Zipping his pants up, he turned to find an amused nurse who took his chart earlier. "Where's the major?"

"Prepping for surgery." She winked at him and ran her finger down his chest. "Thanks for the memories. I'm going to be the envy of all the nurses." In seconds, she left.

Kade questioned the Marine at the exit and was reassured things had calmed down. Relieved, he wondered if he should offer to join the fight or whatever you did in the dark in Afghanistan after an attack. The soldier turned chef returned, reminding him of Rambo on a bad day. He stopped long enough to explain a number of Taliban had been killed and several soldiers were wounded. The others were busy. The soldier continued. "There's a medic tending to our wounded now."

"Not sure they can or should walk," the soldier admitted. "There's a Humvee parked outside the mess hall. I want it, but it won't start. Think you can fix it?"

"I can try. I'll meet you there." Kade hoped he could avoid seeing Vivian who would probably try and stop him.

"Sounds good. I came back for a few supplies. I'll only be a few minutes. Be ready ASAP."

Kade had worked on cars and farm equipment for his grandfather and uncles. He found the Humvee and figured the problem out quickly. They had two batteries, and one was missing. Several sat on the ground next to the car. Kade figured one of the Afghan helpers had dropped the ball because these fine machines were American toys for people with money. Afghans probably shrugged and forgot about it. He finished the installation under the hood on the passenger side by the time the soldier ran out carrying a box of supplies. There were no questions concerning the Humvee, the problem, or a thank-you, just a, "Get in. We gotta go."

CHAPTER 6

Dr. Vivian Palmer threw her bloody gloves and scrubs in the trash then pulled on clean ones. Dr. Wilkins joined her, still wearing his skull cap. He slowly removed his mask that hung from one ear. He moved toward the exit, which was blocked by a big Marine.

"How many soldiers ended up in here, Roy?" Vivian usually called him Dr. Wilkins or Major Wilkins when in the presence of the enlisted men and women. Too tired to care if they were alone, she patted him on the back.

"Five. Two of those were treated and released. They're already back out there. The other three had surface wounds requiring repairs. We'll see in the morning whether they should be shipped out for further assessment. I'm guessing another surgery and physical therapy. They'll live. And General Morgan?"

"A few nasty tears in his shoulder. Probably going to sideline him. I'll watch him tonight for a while, but he's headed to Germany for a specialist to make sure he doesn't lose the use of that arm. Definitely will slow him down, but the big problem will be his temper and refusing to acknowledge anything is wrong."

"That Kade fella turned out to be a big help. Got the wounded back here so Chef Newton could help secure the perimeter." He chuckled. "Fixed that old Humvee, too, and got it running like a new one."

"Where is he, anyway?" Vivian did a visual search as she spoke.

"I heard he went over to the mess hall. Said he planned to make food for the staff here. Come to think of it, I'm starved."

"Hopefully, he didn't undo all I did earlier on those stitches. He got a cut when that Taliban waited for me in my tent."

"What? You'd better explain that part."

Vivian took a deep breath and recounted the story of how there was a dead guy in her tent and why. "Guess I forgot with all the excitement in here. I'm going to need a little help with that."

As she finished, Kade strolled in wearing a bib apron. Vivian wondered if he was trying to cover up his bloody shirt. "I do believe we have a new chef in town, Dr. Wilkins. Wonder what Chef Roy is going to do when he hears a country boy was messing with his knives?"

Dr. Wilkins crossed his arms across his chest. "Not sure. Could be a few amputations coming up. Of course, it depends on what he fixed," he said, twisting his lips as he spoke to Vivian. "What did you fix us, Mr. Country Music Performer of the Year?"

"Grilled cheese sandwiches and tomato soup." Kade raised his chin as if proud of the accomplishment.

Dr. Wilkins dropped his arms then slapped his hands together. "Okay. I'm in. Forget Chef Roy. I'll sew you back together if he cuts anything off, buddy."

"Got it all spread out in the kitchen. I'll stay here with the patients. You guys go ahead. There's a guard at the door and one in the back. Be sure to save them a sandwich or two."

"Deal!" Dr. Wilkins called to a number of the workers who meandered out and followed him across the way to the mess hall. "Are you coming, Major Palmer?"

"I'd better stick around here for a bit." She didn't know why there was an urgency to double-check Kade's well-being again. Maybe it was because she wanted to be near him, hear his voice, and admire his boyish grin. He'd gotten to her in a big way. Never had she ever had a crush like this. Feelings like a high school cheerleader who just got asked to the homecoming dance by the quarterback tingled its way up her spine. Not such a bad sensation.

"Alone at last," he said, walking up to her. "This was one heck of a first date, Major Palmer. Are you always so exciting?"

"It wasn't a date," she reminded him.

"Really? Dinner. A passionate kiss. Wrestling with the competition. And, as a reminder, you told me to strip then to drop my pants. If it wasn't one, I can't wait to actually ask you on a real date when we get back to the States."

Vivian burst out laughing. "If that happens, I'll be sure to take it down a notch or two so I don't scare you off."

He lowered his voice and reached for her hand. "Major, I don't scare easily. I don't know how much time we have before the general forces me to leave, but—"

"Don't make promises you can't possibly keep. I

admit you have certainly cast a spell on my hard heart. But that's all it is. We both know how this will end. You'll go back to all those shiny lights back home, and I'll stay here patching up your fans to return home and buy your music." She dared lift a hand to his cheek. "I really did enjoy the first part of our—date."

Kade pulled her into his arms, and she decided not to resist. "Think whatever you want. I'm not that easy to get rid of. I'll wait for you. Just show up at one of my concerts, in uniform, like all those reels on the internet. I'll jump down off the stage and sweep you off your feet."

"You may have already done that." She stepped out of his embrace when a metal tray clanged to the floor. "I have to check on what's going on in there." Inside the patient ward, she was surprised to see overturned tray tables and supply stands. "What happened here?" she said cautiously, while surveying the room.

Several of the wounded tilted their heads toward a dark corner then patted their bed sheets where she knew they hid a gun. She turned to Kade, who'd followed her in, and whispered, "We have company. Our guard is gone. Go stand next to bed two. He's itching for a fight and has a weapon under his sheet. They all do."

"You stay here. I'll check it out. They need you more than me." He squinted as he tried to appear nonchalant.

"No. Wait," she protested, but he touched her back gently then pushed past her. Her first thoughts concerned the general who lay in the adjoining room hooked up to a lot of equipment. If the enemy still lurked and knew who their special patient might be, his life could be in jeopardy. She avoided Kade's warning glare and slipped in to check on the general.

She'd quickly checked his vitals when heavy breathing came from behind her. She whirled around to see an AK-47 being pointed at her by a scruffy-faced Taliban. His wild eyes and flaring nostrils alerted her to his possible intent to harm. The big surprise came when he spoke English.

"You are a doctor."

She nodded.

He glanced toward a soldier she had ordered to stay with the general. Blood oozed between his fingers that grasped a knife stuck in his gut. His eyes glazed over as he slid to the floor. Without immediate attention, death was imminent.

"I let this patient live, if you come with me. If he has a guard, he must be important. If not, I kill him and the rest. The one on the floor will die soon enough, I think." He pulled back his vest to reveal an American grenade. "Bring supplies."

"I can't help your men if I don't know what is wrong." It took a great deal of strength to remain calm.

"It is not the men. My wife is with child and struggles. She will die if not helped. We do not allow men doctors see our women."

"And if I go, you'll leave my patients here safe?" She had already begun to gather up whatever supplies she could reach and dump them in a backpack. "If you let me bring her here, I'll have a safe, clean place for her. I promise to return her and the child when she is well."

"No," he shouted. "Quickly!"

"If you don't release me when I'm finished, the whole base will rain down such destruction, you cannot survive."

"I will do this." He scowled and nodded vehemently.

He grabbed her arm with his free hand.

His loud voice brought Kade sliding in, gun drawn and murder in his eyes. "There was no one there, Vivian." He froze when he saw the soldier on the floor. "Are you all right?" he growled, leveling his gun at the insurgent.

The insurgent dropped his grip on her arm and nudged the AR-47 into her side. "I kill her if you come closer. Drop the gun now," he said frantically then jabbed her hard enough to make her wince.

"Okay. But if she goes, I go."

"You can't, Kade," Vivian warned. "You're injured. Just let me do this. He'll bring me back."

A lot of activity stirred outside the room, alerting them the medical team had returned. If harm were to come to them, who would treat her patients? She had to escape without endangering everyone else.

"I'll go. Don't hurt the others. However you got in here, let's go back that way."

The insurgent tilted his head toward the opposite end of the room where Vivian knew there was another way out. Usually, it was blocked off with supplies, but they had been sorted and stored in their proper places a few days earlier. A little detail that, tonight, made the difference in survival for these wounded heroes. He backed out with Vivian behind him. At the last second, the Taliban lifted his gun and smiled at Kade.

"No. Please. If you hurt anyone else, I'm not going."

Kade held up his weapon in surrender. "I'll put it right here." He laid it on the floor. "I can assist the doctor if she needs help. Then you let us go."

The insurgent moved his weapon back and forth at

Kade. "You. Take the bag for her. Do not try to be a hero. I might decide to blow your head off. Go. Now."

Several soldiers plowed into the room, weapons aimed. They took a few steps forward until Kade lifted a hand toward them to stop.

"Boys, you don't have a clear shot and you might hit Major Palmer," Kade said cautiously. "Let's not spook this guy. Easy does it."

When the three disappeared through the exit, Kade was ordered to lock the door and push a cabinet over to add time for them to escape. Loud shouts of warning, threats, and banging against the barricaded entrance added to the chaos.

CHAPTER 7

Desert winds kicked up as the open-air vehicles barreled along roads covered in scattered pebbles and unexpected potholes. The bouncing reminded Kade how it felt to be in the boxing ring at the gym he belonged to. Plenty of guys wanted to be the one to knock him down. Staying in shape when you were on the road nine months out of the year gave him the strength to endure concert tours and mindless interviews. Working out gave him the time to escape the unrealistic life he'd chosen. But this jostling of his body, and almost slipping off the rusty seat, caused a jabbing pain he couldn't ignore.

Vivian sat on the floor, between his legs. She hugged her knees, and her head rested forward. The bone-chilling wind smacking against their bodies led him to unzip the oversized jacket that one of the soldiers had loaned him several days earlier. Leaning forward, he scooted down onto the floor behind her and wrapped the jacket around her. She bounced back, and his arms immediately surrounded her. The shared heat from their bodies made the terrifying ride slightly bearable. Both bowed their heads to keep the dust out of their mouths and eyes.

When Kade had to readjust his body from time to time, he took stock of their keepers who rode with them. They had waited outside the medical unit in the darkness, dressed in lab coats, making it possible to blend in at the camp. Once in the trucks, they discarded the bright white coats, revealing the traditional perahan outfit for men in Afghanistan. The lighter colors he'd seen on a few Afghan interpreters since he'd arrived. These guys wore a dark turban, a tunic shirt, and pants.

One of those must have been feeding the Taliban information to provide a way for them to get into the camp. He could kick himself for not being more alert to his surroundings. In the dark, none of these guys looked familiar. To make matters worse, they'd pulled scarves to hide most of their faces. In his imagination, he envisioned them transforming into monsters escaped from a horror movie. Never had he been so scared of the outcome.

They were in danger. There was no guarantee the leader wouldn't torture and kill them when he got whatever he wanted. Would the skills he'd learned on the farm matter here? He took hope when he remembered a famous song, "Country Boys Can Survive" by Hank Williams Jr. Well, that had better be him if he planned to get Vivian out of here alive and unharmed. She wasn't worth as much as a goat to these guys.

"Vivian, do you have a scarf to place over your hair and face."

She nodded.

He found a pair of work gloves in the pocket of the

jacket and handed them to her. "Put these on. Try not to expose any of your skin. I saw a *National Geographic* documentary if women have any exposed skin, it sets them off."

She remained quiet as she covered herself better.

He helped adjust her head covering then she reached up and took his hand in hers.

"Thank you," she whispered. "I'm glad you're here."

He too spoke in a quiet voice. "I think you'd be safer if one of those big Marines had been taken instead of me. I'll do my best. I promise, although I doubt my singing will charm this bunch." Kade could feel her body shake as if holding in laughter in the midst of this horrible situation. He wrapped his arms around her. She nestled back against his embrace and hugged his arms folded around her midriff.

Morning light revealed a hazy glow in the distance. The other men began talking, even joking with each other. It didn't take long to figure out they were approaching their homes. The vehicle picked up speed, bouncing them harder. Dust surrounded them like a bad omen.

At least, since his face remained covered, Kade could breathe. His body, on the other hand, might be paralyzed from sitting on such a hard surface. If he had to save Vivian now, it would be impossible to spring up and attack them. The image of movies where he saw the hero doing exactly that, drove home the conclusion, chances were good you were going to die. If that possibility happened, he planned to be all he could be for Vivian. She didn't deserve this. This woman was important, even to the enemy and these desperate people who wanted a doctor.

"Vivian, wake up. I think we've arrived. Can you stand?"

As the truck came to a stop, most of the men jumped out and immediately were surrounded by old men and children. Women stood in doorways, covered head to toe in black, except for an open band across their eyes. Out here, the modern world didn't exist for women, unlike the ones in Kabul. For a limited time, they enjoyed snippets of freedom not known under the Taliban. Would freedom soon end when the troops left? How long would it be before those women returned to this kind of bondage and invisibility.

Vivian rolled to her knees and extended her hand to him. Kade grabbed it and grunted as he rose.

"We're going to have to make a few rules for any follow-up dates, Vivian."

"Yeah. I'm planning it." She moved to the back of the truck where their captor waited. Surprisingly enough, he extended his hand to her as she jumped down. He stepped aside to let Kade join them.

"I am Ameen. This is my home." He did a visual evaluation of Kade. "I think you are not a soldier, but maybe you act a little like you are." Ameen pointed up and down Kade's body. "Why were you there?"

"I've been volunteering at the medical unit."

"Are you a doctor?"

"No."

"Are you a nurse?"

"No."

Ameen motioned for them to follow him. "So, you are not a soldier, a doctor, or a nurse. The Americans do not have volunteers. Everyone has a job, even the Afghans. They have many jobs to destroy our land and way of life." He stopped shortly. "I ask you again, what is your job?"

For the first time in his life, Kade knew his worth. The Americans, the Afghan helpers, the contractors from home, all brought their special talents to Afghanistan to wipe out the oppression and threat of terrorism. What did he bring? He created music and made millions of dollars.

"I am an American singer sent to give the troops a memory of home."

"And you make money for this?" Ameen's eyes widened, and his voice showed shock.

"I do. But not here. I volunteered to come. I wanted to make a difference." Now that the words fell out of his mouth, they sounded ridiculous.

Another Taliban walked up to them and Vivian stuttered, "Rasheed?" Vivian stepped toward him as he scowled. "Are you okay? What are you doing here. Did they take you last night?"

Rasheed ignored her and handed a flyer to the leader. "This is the man, Ameen. He is a famous music giant in America. He stayed behind to sing."

Ameen glanced over the flyer and smiled. "Are you worth a lot of money?"

"No. He is not," Vivian insisted. "They do not send their best to entertain the troops. These singers hope to get noticed for their good works." She cut her eyes toward Kade. Was she trying to help because hearing her appraisal of his music cut to the quick.

"Ah. I understand." Ameen continued to walk again. "Our friend Rasheed has been working for you and giving us information on how best to get into your camp. He has been helpful." He reached out and looped his arm around the man's shoulders. "Is what he speaks true,

Rasheed?"

"I do not know if he is famous. He sings. The soldiers sometimes sing with him when he plays his…" He demonstrated the strumming of a guitar.

"I think you mean a guitar. One of the men found one and brought it as a souvenir. Maybe you sing for us tonight." They stopped outside one of the mud brick houses. Its wooden door had pieces of animal skin fixed to a few holes. Before Kade could respond to the request, he pulled the door open. "Welcome." Ameen beamed as he ushered them inside.

Vivian, surprised at how clean the house appeared, noticed a window and two other rooms. She spotted a stove and a few shelves in one and guessed the other must have been where everyone slept. They stood on a huge red woven carpet. Around the edges were twin-mattress-size pillows covered in brocade and velvet. She had visited Afghan homes before and they were used for sitting on while taking a meal. They would have been perfect for children to sleep.

"Come. I want you to meet my wife," Ameen declared as he motioned for her to follow.

When Kade came alongside her, Ameen stopped and raised his chin at two men entering from the kitchen. They quickly grabbed him by each arm, pulling him back. His instinct to jerk free caused them to tighten their grip.

"Where she goes, I go." Kade managed to shake his guards off. "You dishonor her by not letting me escort her in front of your men."

"She is an infidel. No one cares about her," Ameen huffed.

"Then why did you bring me here?" she barked. "Take us back, this instant. Drones will be searching for me now. If they find you, they will rain terror down on you like you've never seen before. The special forces will come and show no mercy. Is that what you want for your families?"

Ameen's eyes glazed over as he rubbed his beard slowly. "We will be ready." He smiled. "We are not afraid of the Americans. They will soon be gone from our land and our life can go back to the way it used to be. The British thought they could conquer us, then the Russians, now the Americans." He shrugged. "We always survive. Now. Come. And you, song man, you have nothing to fear for this woman. We need her. She is under my protection as are you if you are her protector."

"He is my assistant, too, when I need one."

Vivian followed Ameen into another section of the house where several children played on the floor. A tiny window and an open door revealed a courtyard. Several other women scurried into yet another area as they passed through to the courtyard. Two more women stared her way. She couldn't help but wonder what they thought of her dressed in what they must have thought were men's clothing and a scarf wrapped loosely around her hair. Even so, auburn strands found their way out to frame her face.

Part of her wanted to push them back beneath the scarf, and the other part wanted the women to understand she was free enough to let her hair and face be revealed. Pulling her shoulders back, she lifted her chin in defiance and dared survey the area like she owned the place. Whether it was in admiration or fear, the women spoke quietly to each other. One of the children, a girl, ran to her mother and pointed at her. The girl, still young enough she was not covered in the traditional burka, seemed fascinated by such boldness.

"In here, Doctor." Ameen pushed the door on the opposite side of the courtyard open. "Please. My wife is heavy with child. She is not well."

Vivian stepped through to this slightly larger space, which resembled the one at the front of the house: cushions around the perimeter and a faded carpet on the floor. It appeared to also be clean. When Kade stepped forward to enter, Ameen held out his arm to block him.

"You cannot go in here where my wives are living. Only the doctor because she is a woman."

"It's okay, Kade. I'll be fine. Wait outside." She wanted to reassure him. His overabundance of concern might get him killed if he picked a fight he couldn't win. "This is their culture and customs. I know it's hard to understand, but it is better if I go alone. Please. I'm not afraid." Vivian touched his arm then withdrew in fear she may be breaking a rule.

He nodded, stepped aside and crossed his arms as if he were a bouncer at a New York City nightclub.

Ameen gruffly added, "She is under my protection. No harm will come to her. You must follow orders. You are alive only because she may need you. Songs do not count for much here."

Kade leveled a steely-eyed show of contempt then leaned against the mud-brick surface on the outside of the room.

Vivian followed Ameen into women's quarters and gave her eyes a few seconds to adjust to the light difference. She resisted showing shock at what she saw.

WHISKEY AND SWEET TEA

CHAPTER 8

Ameen took a step toward a woman sitting on a cushion, back against the wall. Her eyes were closed, and one hand lay across her protruding belly. Several other women in the room also appeared to be pregnant. All but one left the room.

"This is my youngest wife. It will be her first child."

"Youngest wife? How many wives do you have?" Vivian asked as she kneeled by the young woman.

"Just two." He sounded so nonchalant, the urge to frown up at him forced her to take a deep breath and remember she could do nothing to change lives here. Ameen continued, "I have five children, all girls," he sighed with what sounded like disappointment. "Her father promised she would give me a son. In return, he has fewer mouths to feed."

"How good of you," she offered sarcastically.

"Yes. I know. Thank you." He kneeled down next to her.

"And if she has a girl? What will become of her?"

Ameen scowled. "Such things are none of your

concern. I am allowed under Shia law to have four wives." He leaned down near her ear. "Maybe I marry a doctor next time. I think this would solve a lot of problems among my people."

Vivian jerked her face away from his bad breath. She would never forget his odor. "You might want to try making peace with the Americans and educating your women to become doctors."

"Ha. They would become full of themselves and tell the other women they could be whatever they wanted." He touched his young wife's hand on her stomach. "We do not have enough women now to provide us sons, make carpets, and—take care of our needs. They are better to be kept in the dark about the world so they can be safe from the West. Americans gave the women in the city too much freedom and too much education when you came to this land. And we will end it when you leave."

"I should examine your wife. Will you interpret for me?"

He stood. "She can speak English. I will step outside. I do not wish to see her bloated body in the daylight."

Once Ameen left the room, Vivian watched the mother-to-be remove her veil. She wondered if it had been in place because a strange man was outside. She was shocked at her youth. "What is your name?" Vivian tried to smile and remain calm.

"I am Yasmoon." Her attention remained on her hand lying across her belly.

"How old are you?"

All but one of the women had straightened their veils and exited.

"I will soon be fifteen." Yasmoon glanced at the

remaining woman in the room. "She is Ameen's first wife. She is maybe thirty and does not like me. She cannot speak English so will not understand our talk."

The young girl doubled up and moaned. "I have blood coming out. Can you help me have my baby?"

"I am a surgeon, but I did an internship with a doctor who worked with mothers all the time. By the way, my name is Vivian. It's been a long time since I helped bring a life into the world. I will try to do my best, Yasmoon."

"But you are a doctor?" Yasmoon's face paled into a show of panic.

Vivian patted the girl's hand. "Yes. Well, why don't I have a closer look at you." She explained how she planned to examine her, what she needed to do, and how it might feel. Stealing a look at the wife helped her realize how tough this culture was on a woman. Vivian hoped her face didn't reflect her shock at seeing how old thirty looked on a woman here. How long would it be before Yasmoon succumbed to the harshness of this life as well? Vivian offered her a smile and asked Yasmoon to translate what she planned to do so there would be no misunderstanding.

~ ~ ~ ~

Leaning against the mud-brick wall, Kade closed his eyes. It had been twenty-four hours long. How did the military do this life? Vivian worked the day before and then endured the attack on the camp, a threat to her patients, and kidnapping. Add the overnight trip with the threat of possible death by the Taliban and being forced to offer medical treatment without the necessary information and supplies, and anyone's head would be spinning. This woman didn't blink when led into a shadowy room without any expectations of a happy ending.

He never thought he'd ever experience these kinds of emotions over a woman. They had always eluded him. Was this falling in love a kind of worship he felt for Major Vivian Palmer? The gift she carried in those hands saved lives and provided hope for those unable to see past their wounds. It must have taken every ounce of courage and strength she possessed to agree to lead these barbarians away from her patients.

Ameen sauntered outside the room and glanced over at him. "The doctor ask I bring in supplies from the hospital. Come help. I do not know the ones that are fragile and could break. She said you would know by reading the labels on the boxes." Ameen moved away but turned to watch Kade straighten his body to its full six-foot height. "You do not need to worry. She is safe. We bring in the boxes of supplies and put them outside the door. The women can take them inside."

A few men helped unload the truck. It didn't take long to place the boxes near the birthing room where Vivian waited. She came out for a few seconds to find the box with disposable gloves and returned to the dimly lit room. After twenty minutes, she reemerged to speak to Ameen.

"Ameen, your wife is ready to give birth."

"Is she well?" He sounded genuinely concerned.

"No. The baby has not turned so the head will come out first."

Ameen covered his face for a few seconds as if trying to mask his fear. "Will she die with my child?"

"Not if she went to a hospital where there is a lot of

help for situations like this. I have little medicine and supplies here. Most of it is useless for a pregnant woman. Unless the baby turns in the next hour or less, the only way to save them is a Cesarean section."

"I do not know what this is. But we will not go back to the hospital. You must do it here." He looked at Kade as if he didn't trust Vivian. "What say you? Do you know this way to have a baby?"

Kade tried to explain it to him in the simplest way possible according to his own understanding. "It is safe. Here there could be problems because she doesn't have all the help given to mothers duringthis procedure. Ameen, let us take her while there is time. She could die if the baby doesn't turn soon. I speak to you man to man. I know you don't trust the Americans, but they will protect your wife and child. We can bring her back to you."

"The Americans have killed many of our women and children with their bombs, drones, and guns. No. We will not go. The doctor does it here," he snapped. Turning to Vivian, he pointed back into the room. "Go now. If she dies, then Allah has willed it."

"Or maybe Allah has willed that I should be here to save her, Ameen," she pleaded. "If I am to do this, then I want Kade to assist me."

"He is a man and cannot look upon my wife," he insisted.

"I will make a tent so he cannot see her face. Will that make you happy?"

Ameen glared at her, as nostrils flared. "I bring you here to do your job."

"Then let me do it!" she growled, putting her hands on her hips.

He'd taken a threatening step toward her when Kade moved in front of her. "You will not disrespect Dr. Palmer. I will make her pay for speaking this way to you. It is my job. Not yours. Now, will you let me help her, or are you going to let your wife die? It is your decision. You cannot blame this woman who wants to help her if you do not let us work together," he said matter-of-factly. "What is it going to be? Do you hear her pain now?" he said, glancing toward the door. "Be the man your children and people will admire." Kade pulled his shoulders back and glared at the man who controlled the situation.

"Go. You can help her, but I will also hold you responsible if she dies."

Kade grabbed Vivian's arm and jerked her around toward the door. "Get in there, woman, and do your job," he ordered.

Vivian tried to pull free as she leveled an if-looks-could-kill expression. Once inside, he released her and glanced back over his shoulder to see if Ameen would follow. He covered his eyes to avoid seeing the unveiled women.

"That act you just pulled better have been a macho-redneck play, or I'm going to—"

Kade chuckled and kept his eyes covered. "I know I'm in trouble, no matter what. Hopefully, I won't get us killed. Can you set up the tent without my help?"

Her hand slid down his arm and squeezed his fingers. "Remind me to kiss you when we get back to camp."

"Oh, I'm pretty sure you'll do more than that. I have intentions of marrying you, Major Palmer, so you'd better start liking country music before too long."

"Well, I'll have to say that is the most unromantic

marriage proposal a girl could ask for."

"Just say yes, and I'll buy the moon for you."

"I always wanted the moon," she leaned in and whispered.

"You've made me a very happy man, Major. Now get busy so we can get out of here."

CHAPTER 9

The uncomfortable moans and grunts from the young mother-to-be didn't bother Vivian, but the way Kade kept tearing into the boxes of supplies gave her reason to believe the man was nervous. As luck would have it, the Taliban had stolen medicine she could use to do a spinal block for the girl. Maybe she would get a little comfort in the next few minutes.

"Kasmoon, I am going to examine you one more time to make sure where the baby is. Will that be okay with you?"

She nodded behind the veil the second wife held to prevent Kade from seeing Yasmoon. Wife number two left nothing to be seen except a window to her terrified eyes, clouded with tears.

Vivian began a saline IV, and Kade managed to find what appeared to be a coatrack made from a crooked branch and shaved off bark to hang the bag. Together, they quickly pulled a small stand near the cushion where she laid the supplies she planned use.

"Yasmoon, I have good news. The baby has turned,

and we will not have to cut your belly open. How does that sound?" She handed Kade a mask to wear then slipped one on herself.

Yasmoon perspired and tears squeezed out onto her cheeks as a loud cry of pain escaped her throat.

"Okay, folks. It's showtime. Kade, you get ready for the handoff. Are you okay with that?"

"Shoot. I delivered a number of calves and colts growing up. Not my first rodeo."

"Then, why are you pale as a ghost? I can't have you juggling a baby on your way down to the floor."

Kade swallowed hard, rolled his shoulders, then adjusted his mask. "I'm good. I'm good. Yeah. I'm good."

Vivian eyed him suspiciously to make sure he wasn't going to faint. "The wedding is off if you can't keep your act together."

That got his attention as his forehead wrinkled and he squinted.

"Yasmoon, your little one is wanting to come out now," Vivian said. "I want you to push."

A groan filled the room.

"Good girl," Vivian encouraged. "Let's try that again, as hard as you can. The young girl obeyed and added a scream. "I can see the head," Vivian said calmly. "Yasmoon, one more push and your baby is here. Come on. Almost here!"

Vivian couldn't help but smile as she patted the girl's bent legs. "One more time should do it, sweetheart. Ready?"

This time, the baby came sliding out into Vivian's capable hands. She handed the baby to Kade who was waiting with a warm, clean towel. She needed to finish up with Yasmoon and didn't have time to watch the country crooner.

"All done, Yasmoon. You were great. Just going to check you over really good every few hours."

Vivian turned her focus to Kade, who stared at the baby in awe. He lifted his eyes to her and smiled. "I have never seen anything like that before."

"Better than a calf?"

He grinned. "Much better."

"Yasmoon, I'm going to clean your baby then—"

"What did I have, doctor?" Yasmoon asked weakly.

"You had a handsome little boy. Your husband will be very proud." Vivian wiped the sweat from the girl's brow.

Since Kade had moved to the other side of the room, the older wife handed Vivian the curtain to hide the new mother. She gently took the child from Kade to a basin to wash him when his little cries drifted throughout the room.

"Please tell my husband for me, Doctor. I want him to know what a great woman you are." She paused for a few seconds before continuing. "I wanted to be a doctor, but then…"

"I will tell him, Yasmoon. You were very brave."

Kade and Vivian joined Ameen and a few of his men outside the house. The other women who lived in the house were hanging around what had turned into the birthing room. Vivian purposely stopped by the door and removed her mask.

Ameen ignored her and stared at Kade. "Is the child alive?"

"You'll have to ask her. She's the doctor." Kade cringed as he pulled back his shoulders.

"You have a healthy son, Ameen." Vivian smiled at such a joyous occasion, but she couldn't help but think she'd just delivered another male who would treat women like dirt. Maybe his sweet mother would end that cycle.

He shouted the news to the others who also nodded and cheered.

When he started to walk off, Vivian added, "Aren't you going to ask about Yasmoon?"

Ameen shrugged. "Well? Is she alive?"

"Yes. But very weak. She is a child herself. This baby has been hard, very hard on her body. If you want more sons, Ameen, then do not touch her for twelve weeks. She must heal. Do you understand me?" she asked forcefully.

"Twelve weeks is a long time."

"You have another wife," Vivian reminded him. "She will be wanting a son now. I'm sure she will be very happy to have more attention from her husband."

Ameen eyed her from head to toe. "Maybe so. I want to see my son."

He started through the door, but Vivian cut him off. "You must not stay long, and be quiet. The baby may be nursing, and your wife is exhausted. In order for the baby to grow strong, she must be strong. Take good care of her."

"Get out of my way, Doctor." He shoved past her and into the house.

"You're pushing too hard, Vivian." Kade glanced around the area.

"I know. I can't stand how the women in this country are treated. But I don't want to put you in danger too."

He extended his hand as if he would touch her but

withdrew. He stepped closer so their shoulders touched. "I'm not worried about me. What are the chances we have people looking for us?"

"Good. There is a locator in every one of those boxes. They were for medical staff and even soldiers. I activated a couple when we were going through the supplies." She elbowed him good-naturedly. "Make a song out of that one," she teased. "I don't know about you, but I'm hungry."

Ameen returned and faced them. He stared down at his feet for a few seconds and slowly lifted a solemn expression. "You have saved my son. I am grateful. My wife said you tried to make her comfortable, and I know you did not have to do this kindness. Thank you. I will share our food now. You must eat to stay strong. This is a harsh land. We do not have much, but we will share what we have."

"Thank you, Ameen," Kade spoke in a stoic voice. "The doctor is also very tired. We eat then she must rest."

"Of course. And"—he paused and focused on her this time— "a few of the children need to be seen by a doctor." He cleared his throat. "It would please me if you could…"

"I would be happy to do that, Ameen." Vivian gave a slight nod. "This will be an honor."

"Very good. Now we eat. Then rest."

"When will you take us back?" asked Kade.

"When I am ready." Ameen pivoted and hurried off to where the other men were waiting.

~ ~ ~ ~

The sun grew high in the sky as Vivian was given

permission to sit on the floor around what the Afghans call a destarkhwan, that resembled a tablecloth. She whispered to Kade to never step on or over it. In Afghan households, men and women ate separately. Either that wasn't the case here, or they were showing her respect. The women came in and served bread and tea to them. Ameen sat opposite them on the floor. Two other men came to join them and began eating.

Afghan women ate after the men, if there was anything left. She thought of the children and the women who may not have had anything to eat that day. It wasn't unusual for the households to get a meal once a day, twice if they were lucky. Guests were treated like royalty and would not eat on the floor. Therefore, Ameen had accepted them as family. The bread, hard and stale, took the edge off her gurgling stomach. She made a point to saving portions of the food for the women. The idea that she was allowed to eat with the men was humbling.

"Your son should drink lots of milk from Yasmoon. This will happen if you feed her plenty of food. I would be happy to provide for her and the children if you will accept my gift of powdered milk from the army base."

"Do you think I cannot provide for my family, Doctor?" Ameen didn't sound irritated, more interested than anything.

"I know the supplies your people have depended on have been cut off, and crops have done poorly this year. I am a doctor, and it is my wish"—she laid a hand on her chest—"to see your son grow up strong and healthy."

"So, then we can kill and banish the next invaders of our country?" The sarcasm in Ameen's voice bordered on laughter.

Kade interjected. "It is our way to love children, no

matter what country they are from. The doctor has promised to heal people. She is honored among our people. Thank you for taking care of us, Ameen."

Ameen raised his chin in a show of pride. "I will think about your offer. My people are hungry. I am afraid they will become sick as the winter comes."

"Soon, the Americans will be gone," Vivian added. "There will be much turmoil and fighting here. The storage of food will disappear quickly in the cities."

"This is none of your concern. We have survived for hundreds of years without your help, and it will be so again." He stood up. "Now, you rest. The women will take you to their room. I will let your assistant sleep outside. He feels he must protect you, although you are safe. It is good he looks after you, Doctor."

Kade stood and extended a hand to Vivian to pull her up. "Thank you, Ameen. The doctor is appreciative of your hospitality."

Ameen also stood and called for one of the women. "Follow her."

The woman left the two outside a room attached to the central house. One tiny window let in enough light to spot a couple of cushions to lie on. She dragged one out to the corridor for Kade.

"Think you'll be able to sleep?" she asked him.

"As long as I know you're safe, I can. I'm pulling this across the entrance." He proceeded to make himself a barricade as he squatted next to the cushion, now mattress. "I'd feel better about this if I were in there with you."

"Ameen will keep his word. We have done as he asked. For now, we are safe. I'm not sure how much longer we'll have before our people find us. But we have to be ready to go. A few hours' sleep won't hurt. I suspect it will be after dark. I could fall asleep standing up at this point. A nap will do me good. I'll check on Yasmoon and the baby when I've had a little sleep. Thank goodness I didn't have to do a C-section. I'm not sure it would have turned out well for her since I don't have the proper medications and..." Vivian noticed how Kade's eyes had glazed over. She chuckled. "Never mind. Get some sleep." She turned away as he stood up.

"Vivian?" Kade reached out and took her hand, pulling her over the cushion to stand in front of him. She quickly stepped back. "Sorry. I forgot intimacy isn't permitted here. I just wanted you to know what you did today was amazing. You probably hear that all the time. You are one of a kind."

"Actually, I'm not," she whispered then yawned. "Everyone who serves is exactly alike and different in different ways. I'm no big deal. But thanks. I'm also going to have to take a look at your wound before tonight. I'll try and pack a few supplies in my bag."

"I saw a beat-up vehicle out by the side of the compound. I asked one of the men earlier if it ran. He let me get close enough to give it a once-over. I think I can get it running so we can escape."

"Escape to where? It's miles of nothing in every direction. I have no idea where we are."

"Maybe if we got one of those transmitters, it would help the soldiers to locate us."

"Or have a drone blow us up. Let's see how it goes tonight." She tilted her head and continued to smile at his attempt at being her protector. At least he wasn't just a pretty face with a heck of a singing voice. He had guts too. Maybe his bravery was a little uninformed, but she liked that he was looking after her and making a plan. "I do appreciate you sticking by me and staying calm through this nightmare."

Kade took a deep breath and expelled it slowly. "Woman, the only thing that has me rattled is you."

"Whatever. I bet you say that to all your girlfriends."

"Are you saying you're my girlfriend now, Major Palmer? Because I'm good with that." He grinned, staring into her eyes.

"Get some rest, Kade. I'm betting you'll need it in a few hours."

CHAPTER 10

The smell of a cooking fire floated in through the small open window near the ceiling. The urge to continue sleeping kept him between dozing and climbing out of a fog. The dappled light helped him realize sunset must be coming soon. He rolled to his back and tried to remember where he was until he heard a baby crying in the distance.

Bolting upright, he tried to focus on the inside of the dark room. "Vivian?" He rubbed his eyes and his five-o'clock shadow. When she didn't answer, he struggled to his feet like a lazy lion fighting sleep. "Major?" he called softly as he stepped inside the dark room. When his eyes adjusted to the dim light, he took another step. The beam of light from the hall where he slept revealed that Vivian had disappeared.

It took a second to let it sink in after he called her one more time to make sure he hadn't fallen into a nightmare. Adrenaline pumped as he dashed out of the room and backtracked the odd maze of connected rooms in the building Ameen called home. He followed the baby's cries and barreled through the courtyard toward where Yasmoon had given birth.

A guard stood facing him with his arms folded across his chest. Apparently, from the way the man dropped his arms and spoke loudly out of the corner of his mouth, his sudden appearance and demeanor might be construed as threatening. It felt he'd walked into a bar of Hell's Angels who didn't like strangers busting onto their turf.

"I want to see Major Palmer. Now," he growled.

A few more men appeared from another area and spoke to the guard before appraising Kade.

"Doctor," he repeated gruffly.

Ameen appeared in the birthing room doorway, holding his newborn son in his arms. "What is the trouble, country music man. You are loud."

"Where is the major?" He took a sudden step toward Ameen, only to receive a shove from the doorkeeper. Stumbling backward, he tried to steady himself but fell to the ground. "What have you done with her?" he demanded.

Vivian appeared behind Ameen. Her frown and bewildered expression alerted Kade he may have overreacted. Ameen stepped aside and let her pass.

"Keep your voice down," she warned. "The baby is fussy. I don't want anything to upset Yasmoon either. She is terrified something is wrong with the baby. Why are you here?"

"Because I couldn't find you. You should have told me you were coming out."

"I did, an hour ago. You muttered that was fine." She put her hands on her hips in a stubborn stance.

Ameen chuckled and raised his chin at Kade as he spoke to Vivian. "I think he thought we hid you—maybe took you away."

Kade oscillated between being embarrassed at his macho speech and perturbed at her cavalier attitude. "Don't do that again," he warned.

Vivian pursed her lips as her eyebrow arched. "You don't outrank me," she reminded him.

"In this camp, I most certainly do," he snapped.

Ameen was translating the conversation, and his last remark made the rest of the men laugh and elbow each other.

"Westerners give their women too much freedom. This is what happens." Ameen glanced at Vivian then back to him. "Maybe you should stay with us awhile and learn our ways. I think with this one you could use a little help."

"Humph," she grunted as she reached over and took the whimpering baby away from Ameen. "Give me the baby." She bounced and cooed him in spite of the surprised look on Ameen's face.

"Maybe there is something I can do," Kade suggested. Ameen's irritation probably resulted from being a new father. Not so different than any other place. A crying baby had all the control. He looked to Ameen as he stretched his arms out toward Vivian for the baby. "May I?" he asked.

Vivian appeared skeptical but could do nothing when Ameen tilted his head toward Kade to take over. She handed the baby to him and made sure he cradled his head. Kade couldn't help but smile at the little guy and began walking around, gently rocking him against his chest. He had always been good with his nieces and nephews when they were born. To this day, they were overjoyed when he came home for a few days.

The baby fidgeted and puckered his mouth as if he were going to turn up the volume on his protest. Without fear of being mocked, Kade crooned a lullaby. The baby sniffed and opened his eyes wider. He couldn't help but stare down at the little fella and chuckle at the end of the song. Suddenly, the child puckered again, but Kade quickly lapsed into another tune that earned him numerous awards. This time, he included all the verses and quickly moved on to the next big hit in his repertoire. Soon the baby fell asleep in his arms. When he finally looked up, there were children standing around the courtyard with other adults, listening to him sing.

Slowly, he moved back to where Vivian stood, tears in the corners of her eyes. "I'm guessing I can't take him back to his momma, so,"—he handed her the child—"I'll just surrender him to you." Before he did, he couldn't resist a kiss to the child's forehead. "Sleep well, little fella. You're in good hands."

Ameen cleared his throat, drawing Kade's attention. "Thank you." He nodded toward the audience Kade had gathered. "Please. Will you make music for my people tonight? I-I would be grateful."

"I would be honored, Ameen. Your son has removed the heaviness in my heart."

"So be it. You may wait here for the doctor. She has been long time with my wife to make sure she is well."

Kade nodded and found a place to sit on a makeshift bench created from a board and two five-gallon cans near the door. When Vivian joined him, she extended a hand to pull him up.

"You really are something, Mr. Kade Atwood. That baby had been fussy for way too long. He even nursed a little bit a few minutes ago and fell right back to sleep.

Frustration had risen, and Yasmoon was beside herself. I'm pretty convinced they're going to let me go, but you might have earned a permanent place here. Just saying," she said, giving him a fist bump on the arm.

"I hope my audiences don't fall asleep as fast as that little fella did. Not very good for my ego."

Vivian smiled at him for the longest time before she spoke. "That was a beautiful song. Did you write it for someone special? You mentioned the name Rosie."

"I did. When the light hit her blonde hair, it glistened. She had the prettiest legs I ever saw too."

Vivian turned her attention to the ground. "You must have loved her a lot."

"Best horse I ever owned." He chuckled.

Vivian jerked her head up. "Your song was about a horse?"

"Yep. That has to be our little secret, or I might have to give back the Song of the Year award. Promise me."

Vivian couldn't contain her laughter. "Are you kidding me?"

"Tell me you were a little jealous."

She leaned in and whispered, "I was a lot jealous. Never do that to your doctor."

"Yes, ma'am. If it makes you feel any better, I'd pick you over a horse any day of the week."

"Somehow, it does make me feel better." She bumped her shoulder against his. "I have to check out some children. Want to come? I might need a song or two. Think you can make one out of our situation?"

Kade wanted to tell her he already had written an entire album in his head, and it was all because of her.

~ ~ ~ ~

The darkness of Afghanistan masked the hopelessness of the women and children who were destined to live unproductive and repressed lives under the Taliban. At least tonight, as a warm fire burned outside and with a little food to share, a celebration of new life could be enjoyed. A funeral for a baby and his mother would have brought unspeakable consequences to her and Kade. For now, Ameen appeared to be appreciative and kept reminding them they had nothing to fear.

Kade took the time to show the children how to play American baseball. The men got involved along as well. There was laughing, something she'd never heard much from the people outside the city or military bases. Most men wore angry frowns and sinister expressions, while the women moved slowly, covered head to toe in their dark burkas. Being invisible meant a kind of death here. For a short time, listening to the men argue good-naturedly as they played helped her avoid the dread of danger on the horizon.

While Kade demonstrated how to do the cowboy shuffle dance, she stole glances over her shoulder and up at the sky. How much longer would they be here? Their rescuers would do whatever necessary to bring them home, safe and sound. Would these people be hurt in order to achieve a successful rescue?

"Ameen," Vivian said softly as he walked past where she sat on a camp stool. "Can we talk?"

He stared down at her straight-faced. She adjusted her head covering. When she looped it around the bottom part of her face, he turned his attention toward the others then back at her.

"You may speak."

"You must take us back. Tonight. They will find us."

"No. They will not. We move tonight to the caves in the hillside. They cannot find you there. I think they will bring much money for your return. You will tell them we want food and medicine. There are others who need a doctor. I have promised to do this."

"And if I refuse?" She tried to be calm and sound as if it were a normal question.

"Refuse? Women do not refuse me, Doctor." His gruff voice grew amused.

"I am not like your women."

"No, you are not. But you are a healer, so you are of value."

Although it was a risk, Vivian stood and stared straight into his unblinking eyes. "Give your women and children a chance to thrive. Let them go to school and learn a trade to make life easier for the rest of you."

Ameen huffed his disapproval. "Do not put silly ideas in their heads, Doctor. Afghanistan will never change. All the invaders have tried, and all have failed. You will be gone soon, and things will return to what they should be. There will be no food, no medicine, but plenty of broken promises. The Chinese are already making plans to take your place." He chuckled. "They think it will be different with them. I promise you, it will not. We will do to them as we have done to the other empires who crossed our paths." He finally eyed her from head to toe and grinned. "It is good that I like you, or you would already be dead." She opened her mouth to speak, but he held up his hand. "There is no need to thank me." And he moved to where other men huddled talking.

Vivian took a deep breath and let it out slowly so she wouldn't explode. Rolling her eyes upward then to the distance, she saw movement in the darkness.

WHISKEY AND SWEET TEA

CHAPTER 11

Kade surveyed the vehicles sitting idle. What could he do to disable them? He'd overheard Ameen's words concerning leaving tonight. If they kept moving, it would make rescue more difficult for whoever might be searching for them. Although he'd made progress toward not being perceived as the Western Satan, someone dogged each move he took.

The man called Rasheed, who worked at the military base, brought Kade his guitar when he sat down next to Vivian near the fire. Surprised it had not been destroyed, he accepted the offering cautiously.

"Where did this come from?" Kade plucked a few strings as he attempted to tune it.

"You left it in the mess hall, and I took it for a souvenir." Rasheed's forehead wrinkled as he refused to make eye contact. "The soldiers said you were famous, and they liked to hear you sing. I should not have done this. I thought I might sell it to feed my family." He shifted his attention to Vivian. "Major, thank you for doctoring my little girl. I thought she broke her ankle."

"Just a bad sprain. I gave your wife instructions. She should be fine in a few days as long as she stays off it."

"And the others. They are glad you are here to help us, even if they do not tell you. It is hard, and…"

Vivian smiled at him. "I see that, Rasheed. I know you meant me no harm. You are a good man."

"I also know that this will not end well. I tried to tell the others you are important, both of you, and the American soldiers are ruthless when trouble happens to one of their own. These men have not seen the good you have done—only the bad."

"Rasheed, help us escape. Take us back," Vivian suggested quietly. "Bringing us here endangers your family, the children…"

"It is too late." Rasheed's shoulders slumped as he moved away from them. "But please, sing for us one more time. The children and women will enjoy your songs. No matter if they do not understand them."

"Rasheed?" Kade rose to his feet.

The man pivoted back toward him.

"If you'll get me something to write with, I'll sign the guitar. You might get more money for it that way."

The stoic expression on Rasheed's face did not change. Life would never be good for him. He nodded and sauntered off into the darker parts of the compound.

Kade sat back down and plucked away at the guitar, causing a silence to engulf the group. Children tucked themselves into the laps of mothers, and the men hushed their bragging and stared into the fire as Kade sang a lonesome melody. He hoped if he sang loud enough, his music would be the source of finding them. Moon dust swirled across the parched land, carrying a song and a prayer in hopes of rescue.

~ ~ ~ ~

Although Vivian had been sleep-deprived, the nap earlier had recharged her batteries, or maybe it was the anticipation of being rescued. The thought of soldiers rushing in to save her instead of the other way around, forced her senses on high alert. Her body ached, and her muscles were stiff from the last few days. Deep inside, when the adrenaline caused her heart to flutter, she sensed the calvary had been deployed to bring them to safety.

The Taliban fighters closed their eyes from time to time. Their bodies swayed. A few chins dropped on their chests. Never would she have thought music could disarm these dangerous fighters. She checked her watch as Kade sat next to her then leaned the guitar against an overturned cart.

Mothers ushered their children toward the inside of the buildings, a few carrying toddlers. Wearing such encumbering clothes, the women accomplished these tasks in the dark. Did they ever trip and fall into a fire or burn themselves cooking? If she looked beneath the invisibility cloak, which was what she thought of concerning the burka, would she find scarred women covered in bruises?

"Did you notice Rasheed slip away?" Kade squinted toward the darkest part of the camp.

"Probably getting ready to move us. They have to know our people are searching. My guess, the tech guys have locked onto the transponder signal hours ago. I heard something overhead while you were singing. I'm pretty sure it was a drone." Vivian tried not to search the sky again.

"The kind that shoots first and asks questions later?" he asked out of the corner of his mouth.

"No. Surveillance. They want to see who is who and where. They'll be coming in hot and heavy." Vivian chose to sound matter-of-fact, as if it were no big deal. If Kade knew how ghostly and terrifying this would be, he might get in the way. Better if things just unfolded in the perfect dance of the American military. These guys were good at their job.

"Looks like our captors are pretty laid-back right now. Could give us an edge." Kade turned his head. "Wonder where Ameen got to?"

"I promise you; the Taliban is never laid-back. They will shoot us at the first sign of trouble. I've given them what they wanted."

"But they said they wanted to protect you and take you where others need medical care." As he spoke his concern, men rose and carried the boxes of medical supplies to the trucks they'd arrived in the night before.

"We'll be their shields now. If we get killed, it's no skin off their noses. I know you want to believe we have found favor with Ameen's men, but their first priority will be killing as many soldiers as possible and protecting their land. It's just a reality, Kade." Vivian reached out and took his hand. His brow creased, and his body stiffened. "I know you must be confused and maybe don't believe they will go back on their promise. The value of human life is not the same here. The sooner you realize that, the better chance of survival you'll have."

He squeezed her hand and whispered, "There is so much I want to say to you. I never thought I'd meet anyone like you, Vivian. I have no intention of letting you go without a fight."

"If this is the end, Mr. Kade Atwood…"

"Major, I love you. If the worst happens, I want you to know that someone cared and wanted to spend the rest of his life with you."

Tears welled up in her eyes. "We would have been good together. The only men I've said I love you to are the ones in my family. I want to say the words the first time when we are having a nice dinner overlooking a mountain stream where whippoorwills call and fireflies dance."

He placed another hand on hers. "You're worth the wait."

Ameen stormed up to them as three noisy trucks turned over their ignitions, one backfiring, causing many to jump. "Come. You may ride in the front with Rasheed. He is taking the lead." He ran around the front of the truck to Rasheed. "We will follow one at a time, within the hour. We are leaving the women and children here. The Americans won't hurt them if we are gone." He spoke rapidly and kept looking up at the sky then out into the darkness. "Remember, we are all taking different directions to the caves." Rasheed nodded as Ameen reached in and gripped his shoulder. "You have done well, Rasheed. I will not forget."

In seconds, they were on the road. Vivian wondered how much time they had to convince the man to help them.

"Rasheed, what is going on?" Kade asked when he twisted to look behind them." The Taliban are still loading the trucks," he spoke urgently. "If it's money you want, I brought the guitar. It's one of a kind and worth over 27,000 dollars. More, since it belongs to me. Take us back to the base."

Vivian sat between the two men and shivered. The windshield glass had been removed, and frigid night air gushed in. "Rasheed, please listen. The soldiers will find us, and you could be killed. What will become of your family? Who will provide for them?"

He continued to stare out the windshield, leaning forward as if he couldn't see the road. With only one headlight to guide them and the worn-out shocks, the bumpy road caused Kade's injuries to throb. Suddenly, Rasheed slammed on the brakes but remained silent.

"Where are the others, Rasheed?" Kade toned his anxiety down. "Let's go back and get your family and bring them in. The others will be gone soon without anyone knowing. Give them another life."

Finally, Rasheed turned to face them. "And what happens when the Americans leave? Those who worked for them will be tortured and killed. I had to pretend I was a spy to make sure I had a way to protect my wife and children."

Vivian frowned. "The general filed papers for you and your family to go to America. You'll have a new life."

"My life is here!" he snapped. "More important people than me will be at the front of the line. What happens then? I understand these things. You do not. In four months, the Americans evacuate, and our world returns to what it always has been. Ameen did not have to tell me this."

"Where are the others going?" Kade asked again.

"To the caves. They will return to take their families in a few days when the Americans stop searching for Major Palmer and you. I am to take you there too."

"But we're going in the wrong direction," Vivian interjected as she gripped Kade's arm.

"Each of us go a different way to confuse the Americans. I am not going the way Ameen tell me to go. We are on the road back to the base. I disobeyed an order to protect you."

"Rasheed, what about your family? We must go get them," Vivian insisted. "They will kill all of you when they find out."

He tapped on the rear window glass. In seconds, a tarp raised and a woman in a burka holding a small child appeared. Two other wide-eyed children waved at them. "They slipped under the tarp when you were singing, Kade Atwood. Ameen's men took my family several weeks ago, so I had no choice but to do as they said. I convinced them I hated the Americans and would do anything to get rid of you."

Vivian and Kade exchanged concerned glances.

"But that wasn't true," Rasheed said as he motioned for his family to get back down. "I have learned much from your people and have seen that you have better lives. I do not know or understand exactly why, but you do. Major Palmer, you have taught me a skill in medicine, and I wish to continue. I want my daughters to be like you. I don't believe I can do that here after you leave."

"I'm getting you out, Rasheed, if it's the last thing I do." Vivian's heart felt like it would burst. "Thank you."

"Takes a lot of guts to do this, Rasheed." Kade pointed to the guitar resting on the floor between his legs. "Remember, this will give you money for a new start. I have connections too."

A tear pooled in the corner of one eye as Rasheed

dragged his sleeve across his face.

The engine roared to life again, but this time, it jerked forward and coughed fumes out the back. He gunned it and for nearly a mile, the truck acted as if it would be okay until it backfired and stopped.

"Let's take a look," Kade said as if they stopped in front of a Jiffy Lube in Winslow, Arizona. "Do you have a flashlight?"

"Under your seat."

Vivian watched Rasheed jump out and cast a leery stare into the darkness toward the life he was leaving behind.

~ ~ ~ ~

Kade could smell something burning as he lifted the hood of the seen-better-days pickup truck. Smoke and steam hissed upward. Both he and Rasheed tried to fan the area clear. The engine belched a cloud of smoke followed by fingers of fire clawing their way to engulf the compartment.

"Get out of the truck!" He reached in and dragged Vivian out of the cab then raced to the back to help Rasheed rescue his family. Flames spread beneath the truck. The children were crying as they were scooped up by the adults. "Run!" Kade demanded. "We need to get away from the truck."

Ten seconds later, an explosion rocked the night. It created a beacon to their location; a beacon he hoped sent a signal to the American military instead of their captors.

How long would it be before the Taliban found them and made them pay for their disobedience? Rasheed would be executed in front of his family, for sure. What consequences did he and Vivian face for the attempted escape? Maybe he could barter for their freedom if they knew how much he was worth. In reality, Vivian's worth surpassed his millions. She could save lives. The only ace he held at the moment was a scratched-up guitar and a song. His self-worth tanked. The realization that all the awards, hit records, and music skills were worthless in this godforsaken land hit him in the gut. It dawned on him how worthless he was in this situation.

War had a way of teaching you what was important and could put you in your place faster than a speeding bullet inscribed with your name.

The family of Rasheed collapsed after running about three hundred yards. Whether the wife got tangled up in her burka or the children tripped her up, she sprawled on the ground crying for help. He'd kneeled down next to his wife to help her sit up when Vivian and Kade joined him.

"Are you hurt?" Vivian asked her. She'd asked a few more questions before Rasheed interrupted.

"Says her wrist hurts. She won't be able to carry the baby. Major, my children are tired. We must find shelter. Ameen will soon know I did not obey, and he will look for us. The burning truck will leave a bright light to find where we are."

Kade addressed Rasheed as he swung the little boy onto his shoulders. "Rasheed, maybe the oldest can still walk. I'll hold her hand if you can assist your wife."

"Wait." Vivian spun around in a circle, looking up at the sky. "Do you hear that?" She grabbed the youngest child's hand.

"It is the wind," Rasheed said hurriedly as he moved

ahead in the darkness. "Hurry."

Kade came alongside Vivian. "We've got to keep moving, while we still have the energy. Okay?" When she nodded, he lifted his free hand to touch her face. "We can do this, Major."

"I know. I know."

One step then two, no matter how hard, the uneven ground and a mix of grass, holes, and gravel impeded their speed. More than once, the group stumbled, a few fell but managed to scramble back up. Kade didn't know the time, but it felt like they'd been on the road for an eternity. His back hurt from carrying the young boy, and he had to stop often for the girl who took small steps. Add keeping an eye on Vivian, the injuries raging with pain, he began to get confused. Shaking it off would last only so long.

They'd come upon an outcropping of rocks alongside the road. Unloading the children and Rasheed's wife who now limped badly from her fall, the family huddled together exhausted. Thankfully, Kade had pulled several canteens of water from the back of the truck before it was engulfed in flames. He let everyone have a short drink, knowing tomorrow would be hot and dry as the day went on.

"Do you have any idea where we are, Rasheed?" Kade asked.

He handed the canteen back to Kade. "I am not sure. We may have taken a wrong turn. It is hard to tell in the dark, and this is not an area I am familiar with. The last few years, the American military has avoided this way. It is hard to say what the Taliban has done to set traps. I am sure there are mine fields, so we cannot venture off the road. Here is fine because of the rocks. The Taliban learned to keep places safe where they can hide."

"Kade," Vivian said, leading him off to the side so Rasheed could tend to his family. "Considering how long we were in the truck when they kidnapped us, I'd say we are nowhere close to being safe. And we might not be found now that we are away from the Taliban compound."

"Maybe, but I'm thinking that noise I hear coming this way might be our ticket home." Kade squinted up at the night sky.

Vivian cocked her head to listen. "Helicopters!" she gasped. "Sweetest sound I ever heard."

Kade pulled out a transponder button. "Stuck a few from the supply box in my coat pocket."

Vivian fell into his arms and kissed him passionately. "Thank you. Now, if we can let them know we're here."

"Rasheed, gather this dry brush," he called out. "I'm going to make a fire."

"But the Taliban will see us." Even as he spoke, Rasheed did as ordered.

Kade made a pile of brittle brush with dry leaves and twigs. He pulled out a box of matches he'd found when given some freedom to prowl around the camp. He'd also found an old cigarette lighter that still worked and added it to the stash in his pockets.

The first attempt at sparking a fire failed. Vivian helped by using the cigarette lighter and Kade the last match. A tenacle of a flame flared up and in less than a minute, a fire blazed. The helicopter noise grew closer then disappeared into the night.

"Where did they go?" Rasheed asked in a panic.

Vivian checked his wife before responding to him. "They are probably double-checking information, pictures, and coordinates of the transponder."

Then rushing out of the darkness, six combat troops swarmed in around them, leveling their weapons. The children and Rasheed's wife screamed, cowering deeper under the rock overhang. Major Vivian Palmer held up her hands and identified herself then Kade.

"Glad we found you, Major. We were getting pretty anxious about your safety. Picked up your signal not long ago. We swept this area yesterday but found nothing."

"Thanks to Kade, you found us," Vivian said, moving forward to shake the hand of the man in charge. "The Taliban might be circling back. We have to take this family with us. They helped us escape."

One of the soldiers eyed Rasheed. "Major, I believe this man was part of the problem." He moved to handcuff him. Rasheed did not run or refuse but looked longingly at Vivian.

Kade stepped forward and put his hand on the Afghan's shoulder. "We'll straighten this out, Rasheed. I'll make sure your family is okay. Just tell the truth."

"We have to get moving, Major Palmer. We got company two klicks out." The soldier touched his earbud. "The Black Hawk is swinging around to pick us up."

The large Black Hawk was the most beautiful thing Kade had ever seen as it landed on the road. Children were scooped up in spite of their protests, and they ran to take cover in the folds of the power of the United States military. The rotary blades stirred up enough dust that one of the children backed away, rubbing his eyes.

"Our company has arrived. Time to go," ordered the soldier in charge.

"My son!" Rasheed yelled over the noise. "He can't

see us. I must get him."

"No. Get in. I'll do it," one of the soldiers barked as he shoved Rasheed toward the outstretched hands assisting his wife and baby. "Major, you too."

Kade tossed the guitar to someone on the inside and watched Vivian run out to help the soldier. At the same time, rapid fire snapped off the ground and zinged over their heads. "Vivian," he yelled and tried to jump down to get her, but a soldier pulled him back so forcefully he fell onto his back. "Stay out of the way, sir. We got this."

The Black Hawk lifted as the little boy was tossed inside and caught. He tried to crawl forward but was pulled back as both the soldier and Vivian barely made it aboard. She released the grab bar and started to fall back out the door.

"Vivian," he yelled, catching her by the waist of her pants. She was trying to grab the side of the door again when more shots rang out and something sprayed on his face. Kade jerked her inside. The soldier at her side collapsed as well, falling into the helicopter. A medic slammed the door shut. The Black Hawk lifted quickly and turned toward safety. Another helicopter covered their retreat and began shooting at things in the dark. Within seconds, a distant explosion on the ground lit up the night. He could only wonder if it were Ameen.

"We got them." A soldier slapped Kade on the back.

The Afghan passengers were deadly quiet and clinging to each other after such a terrifying event. What he didn't understand was why another soldier, a medic, bent over both the soldier who tried to rescue Rasheed's child and Vivian. Then he saw they were covered in blood. He jerked forward to be near her, but a man bigger than him pulled him back.

"You can't do anything, Mr. Atwood. Let our guy do his job. The major took a hit. Almost lost her. We got about a thirty-five-minute fly time. She's bleeding bad, and so is our guy. The medical staff will be waiting for us when we get back."

"Let me talk to her."

The soldier nudged the medic. "He wants to talk to the major."

The medic leaned back on his heels. "She's out. Hit her in the leg, arm, and side. Don't know for sure, but I'm guessing she's bleeding internally."

"And your guy?" Kade choked as he edged closer.

"The major took most of the hits. He had enough gear on that it probably saved his life. "Know more when we get him to the hospital."

Kade wasn't prepared for what he saw in the night shadows and interior helicopter lights. Vivian was completely covered in blood. Whether it was splatter or she bled from the multiple holes, he felt a sickness well up inside him. He tried to take her hand, but the medic pushed him away.

"No touching. We don't know the extent of her injuries."

"She's gonna make it, though, right?" he asked the medic.

He glanced toward his buddies. "We'll do our best, sir. She has patched all of us up at one time or another. I promise she is a top priority, along with our guy. Okay?"

Kade's breathing became labored as he stared at the ashen face of the woman he wanted to spend the rest of his life with. The hate for all things Taliban surged through him until he thought he would faint from his heart pounding so hard.

~ ~ ~ ~

The trip back remained uneventful until they reached camp. The lights, familiar sounds of military activity, and voices of concern swarmed over them. He tried to jump down out of the helicopter to be with Vivian, but his strength and clarity failed him as several Marines put him on a stretcher and then in a Jeep to head to what he could only hope was a safe place.

The flurry of activity continued as a medical team member cleaned his cuts and bruises. His vitals were taken and then he was hooked up to tubes. He tried to ask, unsuccessfully, what was happening, when Dr. Wilkins came to stand over him.

"We're giving you meds to get a little sleep in a minute or two. You're dehydrated and those injuries need some attention, so I'm going to talk fast. You opened up all those wounds, so when I get a minute, I'll need to go in and take a look before sewing you back up. We'll let you sleep a few hours then if you're up to it, the general wants a full report."

"Major Palmer," he whispered as he could feel his eyelids getting heavy. "Is she okay?"

"We're trying to get her stabilized. She's tough."

"Will she be all right?" His words became slow.

"Might lose her leg. Her hand took a hit too. I think it can be saved but her surgery days may be over. I'll keep you posted."

Kade felt his stomach turn when the doctor yelled for something for him to vomit into. Besides feeling a wet cloth rub across his face and mouth, the only thing he wanted to experience was sleep.

CHAPTER 13

"There you are," said a pretty army nurse Kade remembered seeing days earlier. She had been Vivian's assistant. "I'll tell Major Wilkins you're back with the living. You had a rough couple of days."

Kade tried to push himself up in the bed without success. He tried to replay the rescue and touched his face. Wasn't there blood splatter on his skin when he tried to help Vivian? Where was she? Then he remembered the ashen death color on her body, along with blood splatter, her clothes covered in…

"Good afternoon, Kade," Major Wilkins said drily as he flipped through a chart. "Looks like you're going to live." He looked over the top of the chart at him.

"Good afternoon? That must have been some sleeping sauce you pumped in me last night."

"Last night? That was two days ago. Your initial injury from when you got here busted open during your vacation with the Taliban. It filled with all kinds of moondust, and there were signs a bullet may have gone through you to the other side. Didn't destroy anything important. You'll be fine, but I did have to make sure it had exited, so you'll be sore for about a week." He handed the chart off to the nurse then shoved his hands in his lab coat pockets. "You've got a number of nasty nicks and bruises, so you're patched up, but you will be on a plane out of here tomorrow. Wish I was going with you."

"I want to see Vivian." He threw the covers off, but a jabbing pain landed him back down. Kade groaned as Dr. Wilkins helped him cover up his bare legs.

"Nice try, cowboy, but that's impossible. Vivian is in Germany by now, getting the care she requires. General Morgan wants to see you now that he's on his feet again, though. He'll probably be in soon."

"How is she? Have you heard?"

It didn't take a rocket scientist to figure out all was not well when the doctor momentarily shifted his attention to the nurse who quickly glanced from him to the doctor, then exited without saying a word. Dr. Wilkins pulled a rolling stool over next to the bed and sighed.

"Hmm. Kade, when she left here, she coded."

"Coded. As in died?" Kade forced himself to sit upright.

"The medical staff on the plane revived her. She had a good team. But I'm not going to give it to you easy here. She was hanging on by a thread. Her leg was pretty messed up, along with her arm. I took a couple more bullets out of her before the plane landed to get her out of here. She was critical. All I know, when they landed, she was still alive. Barely."

"How soon can I get out of here and go to her?"

"You're on the next plane, but you're not going to Germany. Your band is back stateside, and that's where you're going. No way the powers that be will let you on base in Germany, much less in the hospital. You've been part of a big pain in the ass, and the high-ranking dudes in Washington believe we were lax in our security because everyone was trying to make a good impression on you."

"Me? I'm nobody."

"I couldn't agree more," came a booming voice from the entrance to his partitioned-off area. It was General Morgan, dressed in uniform and walking with a cane. Tougher than nails, the guy most likely would never give in to a show of weakness. "I should never have let you stay when your band left. I was remiss letting you convince me you could add moral support to my injured men. I regret that decision."

"I never meant to be a burden, General. I only want to do my part." Kade wondered if a knife to his gut would have been easier.

"I understand that. Rasheed told me what he did and why. He is to blame for most of it. I understand that without you, Major Palmer may have disappeared for good or have been subjected to…" He pooched his lips out and shifted his gaze to his feet.

"Rasheed also helped us escape, General Morgan. He was bringing us back at great risk to his own life. If he is ever caught, they will kill him and his family, which they had already promised to do before he helped us."

"I'm aware of that," he snapped. "It doesn't matter. He betrayed us. All he had to do was tell us, and we could have tried to rescue his family. But he chose a different path."

"What will become of him?"

"That is none of your concern."

Kade shook his head. "Major Palmer promised she'd take care of him for his bravery under the threat of torture and death to his family."

"Again, Mr. Atwood. This is not your concern, and the major has plenty of other things to worry about right now if she makes it."

"If?" he growled. "That woman is tougher than most men and has more courage than anyone I've ever met. She'll make it. I know it."

The general took a deep breath then let it out slowly. "I want you to write down everything you remember about the night you were taken until you just woke up. Everything. I'll send someone in later to record your statement of the events. I want a written and recorded account of what happened to see if it lines up with what Rasheed has told us."

"Rasheed was a victim too."

"You'll be shipping out tomorrow, Mr. Atwood."

"Will you let me know any news on Vivian—I mean the major?"

General Morgan eyed him with a sour expression and moved toward the exit. "I'll let Major Palmer know you asked about her."

~ ~ ~ ~

By nightfall, Kade managed to get dressed and could walk on his own. The camp fell into a heavy sound of silence and the people were subdued emotionally. No one asked him to sing, and he didn't have the desire to perform anyway. People barely spoke to him. The camp bustled with activity, packing boxes, dismantling equipment, and carrying damaged goods to the burn piles. Were they getting ready to leave? He had been under the impression it would be months before Afghanistan was evacuated, but maybe the Taliban he'd met were actually scoping out their ability to sweep in sooner. Perhaps if they had managed to keep them as captives, they would have known more. As it was, they were blown up and destroyed.

His thoughts switched to Rasheed and his family. What would happen to them? He tried to find out where he was being held but could never get past the words, "off-limits" or "need to know only." Remembering a map to the camp he'd been given when he arrived to make sure he didn't get lost, he searched through his things in hopes he'd know where the brig might be.

Kade found the location easy enough. A Marine stood guard and refused to give him any information.

"I only want to see Rasheed and tell him I'll do what I can to get him out of here."

"Sorry, Mr. Atwood. Rasheed has been taken for further interrogation at another facility. He's in a lot of trouble."

"What about his family?" Kade asked nervously. "His wife was injured."

"Only General Morgan has that information."

"Then, why are you standing guard?"

"The night of the raid, we took several prisoners. That's all I can tell you. Please, sir, you need to move along."

Kade found a private who agreed to take him to the general and ended back at the medical facility where Major Wilkins was checking him out. He waited to make his presence known in hopes of hearing news on Vivian.

"You're good to go, sir." Dr. Wilkins took a deep breath. "But you should let those hotshots in Germany check you over. You're probably going to need physical therapy."

"Nonsense. I'm fine." The general buttoned up his shirt.

"Well, I'm not signing off on you, so you've got no choice." Kade decided Major Wilkins spoke like a man who needed more sleep and was tired of babying a general who wasn't used to being told what to do. "Any word on Vivian?" the doctor asked as he pulled off his gloves.

"I was wondering the same thing, General," Kade said, pushing into the room.

"Not yet." It was short and to the point. He stood up then displayed his usual frown.

"How about Rasheed? Did our stories line up. Can you see he—"

"Mr. Atwood, you have no idea what is going on in this country, and you have absolutely no skin in the game. Go back to your life and let us sort this out. Be sure you're packed up tonight and ready to go at 0700. Got it?"

"But—"

"Do you require an escort to your quarters?" General Morgan leveled a hardened stare at Kade. It reminded him of a bald eagle ready to snatch his prey out of the water.

"No, sir." When in doubt, show respect. He turned to walk away then remembered the letter in his pocket. He pulled the envelope out and handed it to the general. In large letters on the front was Major Vivian Palmer. "I would appreciate it if you'd give the major this."

The general took the letter and nodded. "Sure," was all the general had to say as he turned and walked out.

CHAPTER 14

Kade's head felt like he'd been hit with a hammer by the time he landed at Hartsfield-Jackson Atlanta International Airport. He'd been forced onto a military transport plane that had all the comforts of riding drunk on a tilt-a-whirl at the county fair. The pain meds he'd been given were generic Tylenol. It wouldn't have mattered what they gave him; there wasn't a medicine to fix what ached deep inside him.

For the first time, he understood what post-traumatic stress disorder meant. Besides depression, he worried about Vivian, the other men and women left behind and, of course, Rasheed's situation. The noises in the airport were frustrating his already irritated temperament. Food tasted rank, and the hustle and bustle jarred his common sense to the point where he constantly scanned the area for problems. His body ran hot and cold at the same time, and he figured he now had a fever.

When he boarded a plane for Nashville, he'd managed to secure a first-class seat. He pulled his hat down low on his forehead and tugged his blue jean jacket high on his neck. He hadn't bothered to shave after being rescued, so he probably wouldn't be recognized. Normally, he loved interacting with fans and tried to be polite and appreciative of their attention. Now, he wanted to be left alone.

His father and mother met him at the airport when he landed. They were shocked at his appearance. His mother fussed that he had grown too thin, and his father asked about his limp and secured a wheelchair, which he did not refuse. Without asking too many questions, they took him home with them and insisted he go to bed to rest until they could find a doctor for the fever.

When the throbbing in his side demanded he wake up, he rolled out of bed and took a shower. He shuffled into the kitchen where his mother busied herself making chicken and dumplings. The aroma filled the whole house. He spotted fried okra on the counter and popped a few pieces into his mouth as his mother broke off a piece of cornbread for him to nibble.

"Kade, someone from Fort Campbell stopped by a couple of hours ago. I guess they tracked you down. He was such a nice young man and even said he attended one of your concerts. Lives in Marshall County and was headed home for a two-week break. I tried to get him to stay for supper, but he was in a hurry to get home. Left this number for you to call. I reckon he thought you were waiting for some information? He wasn't sure you'd be able to reach him, but someone would be on call." She pulled a slip of paper off the refrigerator. She felt his head after handing him the number. "Dr. Cooke is stopping by for supper. He wants to check you over. Why, you're as pale as a ghost. My chicken and dumplings will fix you right up.

"Thanks, Mom," he said, giving her a hug.

He stared at the number for a long time as if it might be encoded with the magical message he wanted to read. Stepping outside on the front porch, he remembered talking to Vivian about sitting on the porch drinking sweet tea. All he wanted right now was a swig of whiskey and lots of good news.

"Hello. This is Kade Atwood. I received a message to call you. A Sergeant Gillispie stopped by earlier, and I was unavailable." The receptionist patched him through to another person who required information from him to make sure they had the right recipient of the message.

"Mr. Atwood, I'm seeing this message for the first time. It comes from the medical staff in Frankfort, Germany. It is sealed. I'm not sure of the meaning, but…"

"Just read it to me."

Kade heard ripping then paper unfolding.

"It's from a General Morgan. All it says is 'I'm sorry. It isn't the news you hoped for.'"

Numbness engulfed him as he processed the words.

"Mr. Atwood? Are you there?"

"Does it say anything else? A number I can reach or a person who I can talk to?"

"That is confidential, and civilians are not privy to this kind of information unless you are family."

"I'm trying to find out about Major Vivian Palmer, who was injured in Afghanistan. I have no idea what that message even means. Does she have family or friends I can reach out to?"

"Again, Mr. Atwood, such information is private. We do that to protect our military because of possible retributions from terrorists. It has nothing to do with you personally. Feel assured that representatives would have been dispatched to notify family when a loved one has lost their lives serving their country."

"That is bullsh—"

"If you have further questions, I suggest you contact General Morgan."

"And how would I do that? Can I have his number?"

"Mr. Atwood, I understand your frustration, but I cannot give out his number. I assumed since he contacted you, you had his location and means of communication. Since it doesn't appear to be the case, this conversation is over. I am sorry the news has upset you, but there is nothing else I can do."

He heard the click of being disconnected. For whatever reason, he kept the phone to his ear, hoping he'd misunderstood or maybe more information would be forthcoming. Nothing happened. Just silence that screamed *the end*.

~ ~ ~ ~

Six months later at Walter Reed Medical Center in Bethesda, Maryland.

General Morgan moved from ward to ward visiting with wounded soldiers recovering from their injuries. Some men and women were going through rehab in various forms, and others were there for follow-up visits. Today was a big day, and he wanted to be there to encourage and support the one person he admired more than any other.

"Hey, you ready for this?" he asked, crossing his arms across his chest as he stared at the woman before him on crutches.

"One hundred percent," Major Vivian Palmer spoke confidently. "I'm finally strong enough and determined enough to do this. Can't let all these guys who came to see me fall on my face for the first time down," she yelled at a few soldiers leaning against the wall grinning at her.

The general noticed a few other soldiers in uniform and maybe six in hospital scrubs, waiting. "Looks like you have a fan club. Kissing up to the officer in hopes for a little sympathy."

Major Palmer smirked and raised her chin at the men who were filing in to watch her slip her new prothesis over her right knee. "I think they're tired of me telling them to suck it up and do the work they have to do to get out of here."

"How many of these guys have asked you out on a date for when they get out of here?"

"All of us, General, sir," called one of the men with two leg protheses. "She's been our cheerleader, so we thought we'd show up for her today."

The general nodded his approval and leaned in to speak softly but loud enough so they could here. "Do they know they have to go through me to be cleared before I'll let that happen?"

"Sir. Yes, sir," they said in unison, standing at attention.

Taking her crutches, the general chuckled and offered her an arm as she lowered herself into a wheelchair. He rolled her toward where her doctors waited patiently then squeezed her shoulder. "You got this, Major Palmer."

She smiled up at him and laid her hand on his. "I don't know what I'd have done without you these past months."

"All I can say is, it's a good thing I outrank those

young bucks who have pulled through because of you. Otherwise, I probably wouldn't have made it out of the lobby to see you. By the way, we have your apartment ready, and one of my men has volunteered to be your assistant until you can drive yourself."

"Thanks, Bud. I appreciate your support."

He came around to face her. "I'm going to stand over there with the Palmer fan club then take those guys to lunch." He turned to walk away. "We'll talk later. Okay?"

The doctors and physical therapist were already surrounding her. She nodded and gave two thumbs-up. His heart ached as his attention fell on one hand, partially bandaged with the fingers fully visible. It had been mangled when she was brought here. He'd seen the X-rays and pictures. It sickened him that a fine surgeon would suffer such an injury and, on top of that, lose the lower portion of her leg.

The only time she'd mentioned Kade Atwood had been to ask if he'd sustained any injuries along with the soldier who had rescued Rasheed's son. He hadn't gone into detail about Rasheed, considering the circumstances in Afghanistan were as bad as he'd ever seen it with the evacuation orders in place. The Taliban had taken back their country, and the people were frantic to leave. He'd mentioned how concerned the country music star had been to not have been able to say goodbye.

"I sent word that I was sorry the news was not what he hoped. I told him about your leg and hand in the message. I had my secretary send an update and how to get in touch with me, but I never heard back, Vivian."

"Probably back on the road making young hearts skip a beat," she said sarcastically. "He's good at that.

Worked on me."

"Look, I think the guy really did like you on some level, but we both know, that place isn't for civilians, and especially not for country music Romeos. Was there something going on between you two?" he asked carefully. "I know it's none of my business."

"More or less infatuation, thinking back on it. He was great under fire and made sure I was safe. He stood up to the Taliban, and that was no easy task. He could've gotten himself killed for such insolence. I'm grateful, is all. Ships passing in the night is all. I'm guessing he'll get a hit song out of it." She laughed. "Hopefully, he wasn't there long enough to have flashbacks and PTSD like the rest of us."

"Why don't you call him? I have his number. Invite him here to speak to our wounded warriors or at least entertain them. I'll bet he would love to see you again."

"Look at me, Bud. I'm a mess emotionally and physically. I would rather him remember me the way I was before the kidnapping. I couldn't stand to see pity on his face or make him feel he owed me something. I would hate that."

"From his recollection of the events, I'm thinking he holds you pretty high on a pedestal. Maybe he just needed time too. Why don't I call him?"

"Absolutely not. When I get on my feet, at least my new feet, I'll think about it. But under no circumstance are you to contact him. Understand?" She pointed her index finger on her good hand toward him.

General Morgan tried to remember how long ago that conversation took place; maybe a year or more? The subject never came up again. He'd seen that Kade Atwood was coming out with a new album next month, and preorders were through the roof already. The album cover would be revealed soon, and he was curious how his Afghanistan experiences would affect his music. Concert tours would begin late summer.

In the meantime, he wanted to do something about Rasheed before the Taliban found out where he was hiding.

CHAPTER 15

Kade Atwood woke gasping, drenched in sweat, and trying to catch his breath. The nightmare played out almost every night. Often, he could climb out of it if he realized what the scenario was about to take place. Other times, he had to surf through it and suffer the crash of helicopters, gunfire, and flashes of light at the end when he woke up.

He swung his naked legs to the side of the bed and buried his face in his hands before glancing at the bedside clock. Brain fog forced him to scrunch his face and try to remember what was on the agenda today. Before Afghanistan, his memory was a steel trap that never forgot anything. Now, he found himself writing a lot of things down on his planner or phone. Most ideas returned after only a few minutes, especially if the coffee was hot and well brewed. When these forgetful moments occurred, he always pondered on those who served in the military and how much worse they had it.

When his black labrador sauntered up with tail wagging and laid his chin on Kade's knee, all seemed to go back into place and feel right with the world. "Thanks, Bluegrass. Should we go have a look at the puppies today?"

After pulling on his ragged jeans, he moved to the small kitchen where the smell of coffee made him take a deep breath and smile. At least he hadn't forgotten to program the coffeemaker the night before. "Come on," he said as Bluegrass beat him to the door. He left it open because the screen door would be enough to keep the chickens or a nosey cat who got tired of working the barn, out.

Kade enjoyed watching Bluegrass run and splash in the creek as he drank his coffee.

This place gave him peace. He'd built the three-bedroom house himself with the help of a few childhood friends. The therapist suggested he get a hobby outside of touring. Remembering how Vivian had wanted a house in the country with porches where she could sip her sweet tea and enjoy nature had provided the incentive to build a place for veterans to get away for a few days. There would be no cost to them.

While they were there, he asked only that they do chores around the ranch. There was a detailed list and a foreman to make sure they knew how to use the equipment. Although it didn't amount to much, the few families who came enjoyed the quiet life, the garden, skipping rocks across the creek, and taking a dip in the water. They could choose to cook their own meals or go to, what Kade called, the grub station.

On the other side of the pasture, various building projects were underway. The vets needing a different kind of therapy worked on those cabins, camped, and were always well fed. If he wasn't touring, he stayed in the house and visited with the men around a campfire after pitching in and working alongside them. He even sang if requested.

Bluegrass came bounding up the steps and sat down beside him. The foreman approached and took off his ball cap before wiping his forehead. "Good to have you back, Kade. It's been a while. Your folks were out the other day to check on things. I think your mom wants one of the puppies." He chuckled. "Your dad wasn't too wild about the idea, since they already have three dogs."

"Well, these puppies are promised to a few veterans already. They'll get training but won't be like the military dogs you're used to. Mostly emotional assist partners, I'm told." His foreman had served in the Gulf War back in the 1990s. "More like companion dogs."

"They could be worth a lot of money if you had them trained for other jobs."

Kade set his cup on the porch railing and joined the foreman. "I don't need any more money. This is much better for me right now."

The foreman nodded and placed his hat back on his head. "You're the boss."

~ ~ ~ ~

Midsummer in Arcadia Valley, Missouri could be brutal; hot, and humid, with mosquitos and periods of drought or monsoons depending on the El Nino wind currents. Combine all that with the beautiful green pines of the Mark Twain National Forest, trails, rafting, and trout fishing, and Major Vivian Palmer couldn't get enough of it. She was stationed at Fort Leonard Wood but made the two-hour drive every weekend to stay with her friend

Fawn in Arcadia Valley. Together, they reconnected over old times growing up, and trash-talked all the mean girls from school who made their lives miserable.

Thankfully, she lived in a cabin on her parents' property, and her new Labrador loved the wide-open spaces. Doggy daycare wasn't ideal but was her only option for now. She planned to go into the reserves and find a practice needing a doctor. That way, she could keep her insurance and still make a difference.

"Hey, how's Mozart?" Fawn asked as the dog rushed up to greet her. After a scratch behind the ears, he took off to play with the rescue dog running out from the corral where the horses were kept. She laughed as Vivian looped her arm through hers. "Why did you name him Mozart, anyway? Funny name for a Lab."

"I learned while I was in Afghanistan that you could sing to Mozart's 40th Symphony." She proceeded to sing, "Put the ball on the golf tee. Let it roll. Let it roll. Let it roll." She laughed. "I thought it was perfect because I'm letting it roll. He keeps me company and gives me something to take care of. I'm glad you talked me into doing it. And," she said, coming about-face, "I found a place that needs a doctor outside Nashville, Tennessee. It's a little town called Lewisburg."

Fawn hugged her friend. "Congratulations. But that means you won't be coming to visit me on the weekends."

"I think that handsome Garrett Horton will be glad he doesn't have competition. You two were meant for each other."

Fawn rolled her eyes. "I think I just threw up in my mouth a little. He's an egotistical jerk with a hero complex. You know he is."

"I know he's a hard worker and a good guy. He always stood up for us nerdy girls in school. We were all in love with him. Lucky his sister was our best friend," Vivian said as she walked toward the front porch. "I see you've closed my favorite place in with screens. Can I sleep out here tonight?"

"You'll be sorry. The whippoorwills are so loud this year. But of course, you can." Fawn opened the screen door and let Vivian inside. "Look at you! You take these steps like it's no big deal. You have made great progress."

"I have. I'm proud of myself. You got any of that sweet tea made for me?"

"Yep. How about we have a glass and catch up on the swing. Your life is so exciting that I can't wait to hear your stories every week. I'll be right back. Oh, did you see my daylilies were blooming?" Fawn pointed to the various hybrids growing along the front of the porch.

"My favorites. They're beautiful."

"I'll be right back, Viv."

Vivian loved it here. She and the other three girls who pretended to be a gang, often came out here to spend the night when they were teens. The smells, the wind through the pines and, of course, the noisy whippoorwills at night, brought back memories that helped soften the struggles in Afghanistan. She still went to a therapist religiously but wasn't sure how much it helped her get over the trauma of war. This place was the best medicine. Maybe if it worked out in Tennessee, she'd finally put down roots.

Fawn returned with the tea and sat in silence for a few minutes. "Oh, did you hear that Kade Atwood was going to be in St. Louis then Branson?" Fawn set her glass down on the windowsill. "We should go since you met him. He has a new album out that is so good. I thought of you because one of the songs is titled 'Whiskey and Sweet Tea.'"

Vivian felt her face flush, and her heart leap to her throat. How could he use their situation to write a song? Didn't he realize how much danger they were in? Guess she wasn't wrong about him using her to get another hit song.

"Vivian, what's wrong?" Fawn placed a hand on her friend's forearm. "Are you all right? Did I say something to hurt you?"

For the first time since she left Afghanistan, Vivian poured her heart out about Kade Atwood and how he'd flirted, courted her, and probably saved her life. Tears didn't spill like she expected, but anger did.

"You fell in love with him." Fawn slipped her arm around Vivian's shoulders. "I know about a guy ruining your life when all you want is to be loved. Guess he and Garrett have a lot in common."

"I didn't mean to drop this on you. Please don't share any of this with the other girls. I'm over him. It just hurts that he disappeared and never looked back. It was pretty intense at the end. All those months of getting stronger, rehab…" Vivian took a long drink of her tea. "Guess I thought, as friends, he'd want to say goodbye."

"He's a big-time celebrity, Viv. Everyone probably wants a piece of him. I read in *Rolling Stone* where he does a lot for veterans, if that is any consolation to you. The military loves him."

"He's definitely charming. Certainly chipped away at my common sense."

Fawn smiled. "That needed to be done. Might as well

have been by Mr. Country Music, as they are calling him. That new album has already gone gold." She pulled her arm back then bumped her shoulder with hers. "Lots of songs now make sense to me. He was singing to you."

"Ha. That's a good one. I'm not ready to listen to it. And I don't want to see him, Fawn," she insisted. "I'll buy you a couple of tickets, and you can take that scoundrel Garrett to the concert."

"Just go with me, Viv. It might do you good."

"I'll think about it."

"No thinking about it. I already bought tickets for St. Louis. We'll make a weekend of it. It's a couple of months away."

"I'm not talking to him and seeking him out."

Fawn shoved her hand out. "Deal!"

Vivian sighed and slipped her wounded hand into hers and felt Fawn's gentle touch. "Deal, my friend. But I go under protest."

Fawn clapped her hands and squealed. "Oh. My. Gosh! I'm so excited to see him."

"At least one of us is. Now where has my dog got to. Mozart!" she called. Kade Atwood wasn't mentioned the rest of the weekend.

CHAPTER 16

"General Morgan, you have a call from that country music guy, Kade Atwood. Says you know him."

The general caught his breath for a few seconds as his secretary waited for him to respond. "Sergeant, get a number where I can reach him. I'm on my way out to a meeting. Tell him it might be tomorrow, but I'll call him."

"Yes, sir."

The general gathered his paperwork and shoved it into a folder then paused. Why call now, he wondered? Curiosity as to what in the world he wanted, troubled him: a favor, an endorsement, let him know some TV show wanted an interview to shine a positive light on his contributions to veterans? Well, he wasn't buying it, nor was he giving any interviews. Not once had he checked on Vivian.

The corporal entered once more and handed him a slip of paper with a phone number. "I also put it on your calendar, sir. He insisted you try to reach him. Wanted to know if one of the Afghans and his family made it out when we withdrew. I told him all I could do was pass the request along to you."

"Insisted?"

"Yes, sir. Insisted. He sounded a little miffed you wouldn't take his call."

"Then it's turned out to be a good day after all. After my meeting, I'm going home." He pivoted to walk out and turned back as an afterthought. "Send Colonel Vivian Palmer two dozen white roses for me and put congratulations on her promotion on the card. Also, send that overgrown puppy of hers treats from that Dog Gone It Bakery in Waynesville. I think it's near the fort where she's stationed. I'll email her tonight if I have any information about Rasheed if she calls."

"If she wants to speak to you, should I put her through to your cell?"

"Absolutely."

"Which reminds me, sir, you had a large envelope with a number of items from your last overseas post. You instructed me to go through it. I found what looks like a letter addressed to Colonel Palmer. It's unopened."

"Envelope?" he quizzed. "Put it on my desk. I'll deal with it later. Might be something one of the soldiers sent her. A get-well card or note of encouragement. She got a lot of those for a while."

"Yes, sir."

General Morgan drove to the Logistics and Strategic Planning Center. There was a running joke that it was a cover for the officers' club and they gave it a fancy title so the enlisted men wouldn't know they were drinking booze and eating all the fattening food their wives forbade at home. It was an amusing idea, but the truth was a lot of intelligence and military campaigns started here.

Rasheed had never been far from his thoughts. When the military attempted to prepare Afghanistan for leaving, he worried about those left behind. Plane after plane took those who had the necessary papers. The numbers had been overwhelming.

The warnings of the Taliban making great progress at storming into Kabul and taking back what they'd lost to the Americans remained astounding. After all the lives and money wasted to improve the third world country and transform it into a democracy, it lay a wasteland, exactly how they'd found it. The women were no better off; that was for sure. And now, so many of the men who had stood by the Americans with a promise of protection, didn't make it out. It sickened him to leave them behind. That wasn't supposed to happen.

"General Morgan, good to see you." A short man from the State Department with deep-set eyes and a receding hairline extended his hand. His bass voice did not match his rather thin body and pale skin. "You remember the director of operations, Lieutenant General Samuel Higgins?"

General Morgan nodded and shook his hand. Although he knew most of them, the introductions continued. The majority he didn't like. He doubted they knew how they were going to fix this problem with those left behind. The new president didn't want his fingerprints on any action that could be perceived as invading again through the back door.

Each took a seat and opened the folder placed at their seat. The general wondered if they'd already read through the information before he got there. Maybe they wanted to appear concerned about the situation by taking a moment to glance over the contents.

"We have a number of Afghans who had their paperwork completed and now have been told that they will not be coming to America. However, several on the list, maybe fifty, have secured passage over the last few months through private contractors who raised money and got them out." Lieutenant General Samuel Higgins tapped his pencil as if bored.

General Morgan leaned forward in his chair. "Then let's pay them to get the others out. It's not like the Pentagon doesn't have the money," he growled. "We can't leave them there. They'll be killed."

"We are aware of that, Morgan," said Lieutenant General Higgins. "There are a possible thirty names before you, which don't account for the family members who also have to be included. We can accommodate twenty of those. The ones highlighted in yellow are those most likely to thrive with relocation. We have volunteers who have left the military and belong to various rescue organizations and will fly in and get them out in a few days."

"My man Rasheed is not one of the twenty. Why?" General Morgan tried to control his temper.

The State Department official cleared his throat. "It's my understanding he caused the Taliban to invade your camp and lives were lost. As a matter of fact, Major Palmer—"

"It's Colonel Palmer now," General Morgan quipped.

"Right. Sorry. It's my understanding she was kidnapped and badly injured because of his actions."

"Rasheed was feeding the Taliban information to mislead them for months on my request. When they took his family, he had to get creative. It happened so fast. They planned to kill his family, and he told them the camp was distracted because of a visiting celebrity, Kade Atwood."

A hush fell over the group as they stared with little to no sympathy at General Morgan.

"We've read the summary of the event and how he tried to bring the kidnapped doctor and singer back with great risk to his own life and family."

"That's right. His service was eight years. Eight," he said, slamming his fist down on the table. "When is the next flight to get these guys out?"

"Not until next spring. That's all we have resources for right now. The new president is looking over our shoulders, so it can't come from our budget. The volunteers' organizations have about run dry," the State Department representative added with his nose in the air. "They're trying to raise money, but we all know the economy isn't great and people don't want to think about Afghanistan. We've been hit with numerous natural disasters this year in different parts of the country. People aren't seeing the importance of bringing planeloads of Afghans into the country to use up more resources."

"Then you shouldn't have promised them Oz when they signed on," General Morgan sneered.

"Now, wait a minute, General Morgan. If you've got a better idea, then share it please," Lieutenant General Higgins snapped.

"What if I know someone who can get in and out to rescue the rest of the ones on the list, including Rasheed?" General Morgan closed his file folder carefully.

"By all means, knock yourself out. We'll share the intel and plan if you can pull it off by the time we lift off in two weeks."

General Morgan stood. "Consider it done."

He couldn't get out of the meeting fast enough and drove like a bat out of hell to his office. His secretary jumped up to salute when he walked in but was waved off. "Get me that Atwood guy on the phone ASAP. I want a secure line too. Can you do that for me?"

"Yes, sir."

"Don't take no for an answer either. Tell him I've got news he'll want to hear."

Five minutes later, Kade Atwood was patched in on a secure line. A few minutes of pleasantries commenced then transitioned to the work the country music star was doing on behalf of the veterans and their families.

"I wouldn't be surprised if you didn't get nominated for the Presidential Medal of Freedom, Kade. I've heard a lot of good things about you."

"Thanks. The reason I called earlier was to check if Rasheed and his family got out. I've tried to find out without bothering you, but I haven't had any luck. I know that was something Major Palmer wanted and promised him. It's been over a year now. Is he okay?"

The general was going to not give him the benefit of knowing Vivian had been promoted. "Rasheed shared as much, and I tried. Unfortunately, I have not been successful at getting him out."

"He's still there?" Kade asked in bewilderment. "Is he alive?"

"As of three days ago, he was. There's one more plane flying under the radar to pick up twenty families in two weeks. An all-volunteer crew made up of ex-military.

However, Rasheed isn't one of those slotted to go, due to his collaboration with the Taliban. The committee said he used you as an excuse to invade the camp, thinking security would be lax."

There was silence on the other end of the phone for a few seconds. "So, I'm the bad guy here? It's all my fault?"

"I never said that. Rasheed had been feeding the Taliban false information we gave him for months. They began to get suspicious and took his family. Ameen wanted a doctor to help his pregnant wife, so they took his family and gave him an ultimatum. It happened quickly, and the man was scared out of his mind they'd kill his family. Without telling me what had happened, he mentioned you and the possibility of a good time to sneak in."

"But he watched after us and—"

"You're preaching to the choir, Atwood. Unless we get him out in the next two weeks, it will be spring before any more rescues can take place, no matter if the paperwork is completed or not. There just is not enough manpower, money, or a plane to get them out."

"I can help," he said hurriedly. "I've made friends among the ex-military and special forces guys, and I bet they can find a plane and pilot."

"Doesn't matter. The relief organizations have run out of money."

"I'll pay for it. All of it. I don't care what it costs."

"You might if you knew the price tag." The general sat on the edge of his desk and switched ears with the phone.

"Shoot me a number. In the meantime, I'll go online and set up a GoFundMe page for Afghan relief and rescue. Tell me who and what you need."

"Can you get this information in forty-eight hours so I can put it in front of the bigwigs who gives us a go? Can you do that?"

"Yes. Is this the number where I can reach you?"

"This number is the most secure. It's best if we do it that way."

"Thanks for this opportunity, General Morgan."

Kade clicked off, and the general dared feel a glimmer of hope.

Then the sergeant came into the office. "Did you make progress, sir?"

General Morgan smiled and stood. "I think we're in business, Corporal. Thanks for sticking around. I have a few more things I want you to get ready for my Zoom meeting presentation with the DC bunch in a couple of days.

CHAPTER 17

General Morgan waited a few seconds for Kade to answer his call. The guy had managed to pull it off, getting the necessary funds, support team, and a plane for a rescue trip to Afghanistan. The people who were going had done the operation earlier in the year and understood the logistics, danger, and possible outcomes of the trip. The volunteers who took time off from their jobs included former military, intelligence, and diplomatic personnel.

Not only had the country star paid for most of the trip, but he'd secured a number of other donors who promised to keep the momentum going to get another plane into Afghanistan in the next two months. The man was relentless in finding the right people.

He once asked if he could tag along, but the general shut that down immediately with about ten reasons why not. Fortunately, the singer was smart enough to understand that he would have been yet another security matter and too many chances to let such information fall into the wrong hands. With him along, the whole trip would have been jeopardized and had to be scrapped.

"General?" Kade asked anxiously.

"Just wanted you to know wheels are up, and they are on their way. There's going to be a stretch of time they'll go dark and we won't hear anything."

"What is the turnaround time?" Kade asked.

"A rescue mission in Afghanistan can take a few days or several weeks to complete. This one may have a degree of complexity to the operation since the Taliban is pretty locked in by now and doesn't want us poking our nose into their business. Also, the location within the country and the security situation is important. There, you never know. A typical timeframe for a high-priority rescue mission would likely be a few weeks. Those guys you got know their stuff and are prepared to extend the mission if there are hiccups. I know you're anxious to see this to completion. I have the Pentagon breathing down my collar because there are no active military there now, and if these guys get into trouble, then they're on their own."

"I'm working on places in the States for the people on the second plane to stay and get assimilated."

"Good. They've been vetted and approved, so hopefully nothing major goes wrong. Expect a couple of weeks before they're back, but it could be sooner. Weather also plays a part in this. Those Afghans are terrified out of their minds right now, and we are their only hope," the general reminded him.

"Thank you, General Morgan, for letting me help and keeping me in the loop. I've worried about them since I left there. Major Palmer would be pleased."

The general didn't respond to the last remark. The man still hadn't asked about her, and it sickened him.

Then out of the blue, after clearing his throat, he stuttered," I-I still miss her. I wish we'd had more time." Voices called to him in the background, and he finished up quickly. "Thanks again, General. Call me when you have news."

"Will do, Kade. This has to stay under your hat. Don't be talking about it to anyone," the general warned.

"I understand. Until next time."

General Morgan clicked off, and the general leaned back in his swivel chair. Once again, he pulled out the top drawer and took out the envelope Kade had given him before he left Afghanistan. Part of him wanted to open it and check if there was anything to upset Vivian. She'd been through so much. Could it be a Dear John letter or a *thanks for the memories,* kind of note? It didn't add up. The two of them had gone through a traumatic experience together, and he had never checked on her. The general could have sworn more was brewing between them than survival.

After all Kade had done for this rescue mission, and other projects for military families, he owed it to the guy to give Vivian the letter, no matter what it said. Maybe it would be the closure she needed.

~ ~ ~ ~

Kade held the phone to his chest for a few seconds, letting his heartbeat slow enough in order to breathe naturally. It all had come rushing back to him while talking to the general. Memories of singing to the wounded and the others who served, the flirting with Vivian Palmer and getting to know her, flooded his senses. The unexpected jolt of falling in love with a woman he'd never be able to make his own because of a group of men who hated freedom still confused him. They hated the US and anything that went against their interpretation of right and wrong. The kidnapping and the possibility of death affected him less now. But times like these, he remembered how close to being killed he came.

The nightmare replayed way too often. He could see clearly Vivian getting shot multiple times and nearly falling out of the helicopter. The blood-covered body, the sound of the rapid fire, the rotary blades of the Black Hawk, the loud voices, and the orders to get out of the way still haunted him. A big regret was not being able to see her before she was whisked away to Germany. By the time he reached the States, his Vivian was gone—forever.

How many days had he faced complete devastation, knowing he'd never hold her again or feel the softness of her skin?

How many days had it taken him to heal enough to put one foot in front of the other, knowing others had it worse than him, yet he survived?

How long would the survivor guilt last if he drank one more shot of whiskey?

How long did it take to begin writing music again to help heal his heart that felt like it carried bullet holes left by an enemy who didn't consider how Vivian had saved Taliban lives without caring who they were.

The one thing that took the edge off was volunteering for veteran and troop events. Building the shelters for families in Tennessee for them to have a few days of relaxing time in nature had been therapeutic—for the most part. But each time he sat on the front porch, he thought of Vivian and how she would have loved it.

Her death had hit him so incredibly hard. He thought his contacts might have located where she was buried or family he could reach, but the military told him the information remained confidential. It didn't matter if he was Kade Atwood. The information wasn't going to be given out to him.

He tried to see if she'd been buried at Arlington National Cemetery, but that, too, ended up leading him nowhere. Finally, he gave up. The outcome would still be the same: She died. Maybe, by writing her songs, he could express the impact she had on his life. The one thing he wanted to accomplish was to complete Vivian's promise to Rasheed. Maybe then he could move forward.

When Kade's assistant entered the room, he tapped the tablet she carried. "Contact whoever you need to about our concert in St. Louis. It's in August for two nights." By then, he'd know if Rasheed had made it out of Afghanistan and started a new life, which he also intended to make happen. "Send General Bud Morgan free tickets for him and guests. Box seats. Provide the hotel—whatever you think they'll need. I know there's an army base a couple hours from there. I'm sure he'll know how to distribute the tickets. Just make sure he's there. I don't think he likes me very much, but I'm trying to make amends by helping out his men."

"Of course," the secretary replied. "You do so much. I doubt he dislikes you."

"He's military through and through. To him, I'm just a country boy who can sing. He believes I'm a celebrity who is used to getting my way on absolutely everything."

"Well, aren't you?" She smiled as she programed the dates and instructions into the tablet.

He chuckled. "Maybe. But hopefully, I can make a difference."

"You're a good man, Kade." She slowly zeroed in on his face and gave him a coy expression that had started to be more frequent.

He nodded and thanked her as he moved away to the stage being readied for the night's performance. As lonely and empty as he felt most days, getting involved with someone else wasn't what he wanted at the moment. Those shy glances of interest, groupie mentality, and an abundance of fakeness had been prevalent in his life for too long. Vivian had changed how he saw the world, what it meant to be real and a contributor rather than a user.

It was always Vivian.

~ ~ ~ ~

The two planes sat on the runway at Mazar-e Sharif in the fifth largest city of Afghanistan. General Morgan had technical support following the rescue team's progress from the beginning. In order to land, the Taliban had insisted on more humanitarian aid, that included medical and food supplies. It had been anticipated, given that twenty million people throughout Afghanistan were in desperate need of day-to-day necessities and considered suffering from food insecurity. Recently, it had gotten the deserved title of the most unhappy country in the world.

The ambassador of Qatar and other officials from Turkey had been working around the clock to reestablish contact with the 300,000 Afghans in this part of Afghanistan. The economic puzzle pieces required repairing the runways, restoring radar, and getting the fuel for planes in order to schedule flights with lifesaving supplies. Hopefully this would abort widespread disease and starvation. This particular rescue mission would be the first for this area.

Mazar-i-Sharif, located in close proximity to both Uzbekistan and Tajikistan was considered the regional hub of northern Afghanistan. Upon leaving, the crew knew if anything went wrong, there would be a group people in Uzbekistan standing by to service the plane or deal with other problems. Since the small country lay thirty-four miles from the Afghanistan border, confidence was high on a successful handoff of the vetted Afghans leaving the country.

"What's the holdup?" General Morgan asked the leader of the mission sternly.

"Just waiting for the signal to open up the plane and a designated person to get the supplies. Airport security insisted we wait until protection could be provided for the supplies. I notice activity now. There's a lot of yelling and arguing between a few Taliban guys and locals. I'll get back to you, General Morgan. No sweat. This happens."

The line went silent, and there was no recourse but to wait. Maybe he'd call Vivian and give her the news, but he thought better of it. If this ended up on the bad side of hope, he didn't want to hand her another disappointment.

An hour later, he got the expected call. "General, we have a problem."

CHAPTER 18

The weekends spent back in Arcadia Valley with her friend Fawn gave Vivian a chance to be normal again. She'd even tried hiking a few trails in Red Bluff Park where she and Fawn used to go swimming with their little gang of misfits. Together, they leaned on each other to vent about the men in their lives and laugh at their silly and sometimes dangerous antics.

But the time came when she traveled to Tennessee to meet her new team of medical professionals and get a feel for the land. The physician position at a new clinic catered to veterans but also the surrounding area. She dreaded moving away from the safety of Fawn and everything else embedded in her life. Taking a few extra days to explore gave yet another element to being independent again. Now that she'd gained back the confidence she'd lost in Afghanistan, maybe she could complete the adjustment to losing a leg and living with a damaged hand that might prevent her from ever doing surgery again.

The administrator of the clinic was retired military and specialized in public health and counseling. He expressed appreciation of the fact that Vivian would require several more surgeries on her hand if she planned to ever do what she loved most. Thankfully, he had found a place for doggy daycare while she got acquainted with the staff and her surroundings and options for a new life.

"I know you said you'd be here a couple more days before going back to Fort Leonard Wood. Hope you like it here." The administrator shoved his hands into the pockets of his lab coat.

"This area reminds me of the Missouri Ozarks. Makes me feel right at home. Everyone is so friendly, Major Tindel."

"Please, call me Mac. I'm out of the military now. Besides, you outrank me." He laughed. "My wife suggested I reserve a few days at the Let It Roll Camp down the road. It was built by wealthy donors, I think. Veterans can bring their families for free and enjoy nature, experience farm life, and get away from the ghosts that haunt them. Several have come back to help build more cabins. My wife was able to get you the main house. It has three bedrooms, kitchen, everything you'd want. I didn't know if you'd be bringing anyone with you. We thought you might want a place to sort things out."

"You tell Katie I appreciate it. Can I take my dog?"

"Very dog friendly. As a matter of fact, they raise Labs for emotional assist dogs."

"Really?" Could this be where Mozart came from? "What's the name of the kennel?"

"I'm not sure. Anyway, your reservations are for the next two nights. Going to be pretty for a few days, but storms expected later in the week." He stuck out his hand. "I'm so glad you're coming to be a part of our team, Colonel Palmer." He spoke very officially.

With a grin, she leaned in and took his hand. "Call me Vivian when it's just us."

"Will do." He walked her out to her car. "Guess I'll see you in a few months. I'll keep my ears open for a place for you to live."

By the time she'd picked up her dog and arrived at Let It Roll Camp, the sun dipped toward the horizon. The place took her breath away. The white-framed house with its wraparound porch was everything she dreamed of owning. Mozart bounded out of the car and ran to the creek that glimmered with the sinking sun. The quiet tumble of low rapids invited her to toss a stick for Mozart. Joyfully, he jumped into the clear water, searching for the prize. Once he'd found it, he loped back to Vivian, shaking his wet body as part of the gift. Laughter escaped her as she sucked in a deep breath of clean air and admired the gentle sway of the willows on the opposite bank of the creek.

"Okay, boy, we have to get settled in for the next few days. I'm beat. Besides, I want time on that front porch."

A note and an envelope of instructions were attached to the front door. Included were phone numbers in case of an emergency, a map of the property, Wi-Fi information, and options for food service if required.

Unlocking the door, she refused to let Mozart inside until she grabbed a hand towel and wiped him down. She took a few moments to inspect the house and fell in love. Parts of it reminded her of Fawn's little cabin in Arcadia Valley and others of her own home growing up. The furnishings had been kept simple. The hardwood floors shone, and, the sheer curtains and comfy chairs begged her to read a book or watch a movie.

"Let's check the fridge, Mozart. Maybe we'll have to check out the cafeteria." Delighted to find fresh pasta that only needed warming, she stuck it in the oven. The French bread wrapped in foil needed only a little warming. The premade salad had been provided, like the entrée, in a disposable container. A canister of tea bags sat next to the stove, so she quickly made her drink of choice.

The camp phone on the counter rang several times. "Hello?"

"Oh good. You made it. I'm Bobby Joe, and I'm tied up out of town. I had a puppy that needed to be rescued, one of our former dogs. The owner could no longer take care of her, so I'm bringing her home. But, as luck would have it, my truck broke down in Knoxville."

"Not a problem. Your instructions were clear and very helpful. I noticed you have other dogs in kennels. Do I need to feed them?"

"No. A couple staying there this week is taking care of that. It's their job during their stay. Just wanted you to know so you wouldn't be concerned about possible strangers on the property. Mary and Rick Jennings. Good folks. Hope you enjoy your stay."

Taking the time to make sure there were no surprises for a former combat soldier was a nice touch. Sudden noises, strangers, and shadows still could set her off if she wasn't vigilant.

"Thank you. I love it already."

Making dinner took only a few minutes, and she decided to eat on the front porch. When the Jennings showed up to take care of the dogs, they stopped to make sure she knew why they were there. It didn't take them long in the kennels, and Mozart tried to tag along to help. He wasn't allowed in the barn with the other dogs but made friends with Rick and Mary nonetheless. They walked him back to her to ensure he didn't follow them across the pasture to where they were staying.

"Where did you get your dog?" Mary asked. "He sure is friendly."

"A place called Dog Tags, or so I was told. I went through a friend at Fort Leonard Wood. She patted her prothesis. "Had a rough time for a while, and Mozart saved my life."

Mary and Rick chuckled.

"Well, for your information, this kennel is Dog Tags. Isn't that crazy?" Rick asked as he patted Mozart on the head.

"You're kidding? I didn't care where he came from at first, I was just so glad to have him. I wish I could meet the owner to thank him for doing this for vets and the wounded. It means a lot to me."

They talked a little while longer then decided to head back before it got dark, letting her know they'd be back tomorrow to clean up the kennels then again to feed at night. For the first time in a long time, Vivian felt at peace being alone.

She slept through the night without a nightmare and enjoyed the morning breezes coming through the screens at sunrise. Early morning coffee on the porch, sitting in a rocking chair, listening to the birds convinced her she'd landed in Nirvana. The decision to take the new job now became a life choice she anticipated with joy rather than dread of one more adjustment. Mozart sprawled on the porch for his first of several morning naps. Future plans: save her money for a place like this. It would be a dream come true, and what else could she possibly want?

Maybe a special person would burst into her life again, someone who wanted a person who was still a little broken but showed great promise. In the meantime, she decided to break down and try to find Kade Atwood's latest album. What was she afraid of anyway? How could a few songs make a difference?

~ ~ ~ ~

General Morgan slowly sat down in his chair and rolled up closer to the desk. "What's going on, Dillon? Everyone okay?"

"Yeah. Taliban are pissed off about something. We just got everything off loaded, and we're refueled. We have the money ready to pay off the right people. The Taliban are searching for something or someone. They're stopping the Afghans slotted to leave and trying to intimidate them. A few of my guys are in there now trying to counteract that intimidation. The Ts don't understand anything but violence and brutal control."

"What's the plan?" The general thought his blood pressure had kicked up, since his face had gotten hot and his head began to pound.

"My guys are returning the supplies to the plane. The locals are having a meltdown and threatening the Taliban with their own methods of intimidation. I have someone to interpret for us, so we're getting it pretty straight. The real problem is they're looking for a man named Rasheed."

"We can't let that happen." The general rubbed his

pinched brow to make the strengthening headache disappear.

"No, sir. It's my understanding many of the passengers have new names and identities. However, if any of his enemies are here, they may recognize him." Dillion paused to speak to a person in the background.

"He's a dead man if he doesn't get on that plane, Dillion," General Morgan insisted.

"Okay. Now it looks like we're moving the supplies back into the airport. We're going to wait until the middle of the night to load passengers on the plane. The Taliban will be tired, maybe high with any luck, and we can begin to check papers, passports, and get them loaded. The kids will be sleepy and not likely to be scared and start crying."

"Think this will work?" The general let out a sigh.

"That Rasheed guy must be pretty important for you to take such an interest."

"They all are, Dillion."

"Roger that, sir. I hear ya. We'll do our best. It might be morning your time before you hear from me again. The cash speaks volumes with these guys."

"Thanks. I know you'll do your best."

~ ~ ~ ~

Kade noticed he'd missed a call from his foreman, Bobby Joe. He'd hoped it was information on the Afghanistan rescue. Checking his watch, he realized he was trying to rush a dangerous and impossible mission. Taking a deep breath, he called the foreman.

"Bobby Joe, sorry I missed your call earlier. What's up?"

The foreman informed him about the rescue dog and that he'd try and place her as soon as possible. There was a quick rundown of the progress of the last cabin expected to be ready by September.

"I couldn't be there for the arrival of a new guest at the house built for you when you're here. Hopefully, I'll make it back in time to get acquainted like we always do. I know you expect a full report. The new veteran's clinic in Lewisburg made the reservations. Dr. Mac, I think."

"Oh yeah. I know Mac. Great guy. I'm sure whoever is there will be fine. Do you remember the name?" Kade propped the phone between his ear and shoulder as he checked his calendar.

"No, sorry. It was a colonel though. Never had a high-ranking officer before, that I know of. I don't have my notebook with me. Left it in the truck." Bobby Joe moaned.

"You can tell me later. I like to have an idea of what the guests like and will they come back. Might build a second one. I'm thinking I should build another place away from there since it's turning into a popular place to stay for a few days, especially for families. Probably why the colonel stayed there. We'll discuss when I get home. Thanks for taking care of the rescue dog. I'm sure we'll find another home for her."

"I'll head back tomorrow if my truck gets fixed. The tour going okay?"

"Yes. But I'm already tired. Going to take a few days off. I want to come home and talk to Mac at the clinic about a medical program to train vets or even Afghan refugees who qualify. He might have more ideas about where to get funding."

"You're spreading yourself pretty thin, Kade," Bobby

Joe scolded. "Maybe slow down and rest for a few days. I'll pick you up at the airport in Nashville when you're ready."

"Might be day after tomorrow."

"Sounds good."

CHAPTER 19

Rain bounced off the tin roof of the charming house Vivian had fallen in love with. She stood in the doorway, letting the breeze tease her skin as it pushed through the screen door. Lightning flashed across the sky like spider legs, followed by the rumble of thunder. In the background, Kade Atwood's music from his latest album played for the fifth time that day. Tears rolled down her cheeks as she hugged her arms against the mist that moved onto the front porch and into the house. Shutting the door, she swiped her sleeve against her face and hurried to shut the windows against the blowing rain.

Mozart rose to his feet and followed, as if he were making sure she was okay. She reached down and rubbed behind his ears. "What would I do without you, Mozart? I think I've had enough of Kade Atwood for one day." She turned the music app on her cell phone off only to have the cover of the album pop up. And there he was: unruly hair and intense eyes staring out into the distance. Afghanistan. The whole album had themes that were gut-wrenching for someone who had been through war. She could imagine people who hadn't pulled out their credit card and donated to the nearest military charity, VFW, or VA hospital.

But one song ripped at her heart: "Whiskey and Sweet Tea." Basically, it was about falling in love with a girl waiting for him on the front porch back home. A tsunami of flashbacks slammed into her tough side until she had to admit he broke her heart when he didn't try to reach her through the worst days of her life. Apparently, Afghanistan was great at creating false impressions and relationships. Then, let a little thing like losing part of a leg or destroying one of your surgical hands, a life together didn't look nearly as pretty or sustainable. A hotshot celebrity certainly wouldn't want a cripple on his arm when he received another Grammy or country music award.

"I'm bigger and better than this, Mozart." Vivian knelt next to him and hugged his neck. "This place made me let my guard down. I'll be fine in the morning." She rose. "Come on. Let's call it a night. Rainy nights always make a person sleep like a baby." A laugh escaped her. "Now that really does sound like a country song. Think I can write one?" The dog tilted his head as if he knew a question had been posed to him. He answered with a loud bark.

The following morning reminded Vivian of a landscape that had been scrubbed clean. The air smelled fresh, and crystal droplets still fell recklessly from the trees when a breeze teased the branches. The coolness would soon be overtaken by the heat and humidity that came with Tennessee summers.

The darkness that threatened her mental stability the

night before had evaporated after another good night's sleep. She and Mozart strolled down to the creek. The temptation to skip rocks across the whispering rapids as she'd done as a child was too great to resist. She was happy her hand would cooperate and her skipping improved with each cast.

Later, she circled back to the kennels to visit with four Labs in their outside runs. They were currently running around nearly an acre of fenced land and enjoying the sun. The kennels had a doggy door for them to return inside if they preferred a cooler spot. She'd read a pamphlet left for her about how the kennels were kept cool in the summer. There was no mention of who the owners were, except that they had a heart for the military and wanted to make sure each puppy went to a deserving family. A Dog Tag Kennel Fund had its own Facebook page, and donations were appreciated.

She made a mental note to make a monthly donation after reading a pamphlet detailing the resort, created by a wealthy Tennessean, for vets to have a safe place to rest. There were also apprenticeships for mechanics, carpenters, electricians, HVAC, and plumbing programs partnered with a local technical college. Again, no mention of who initiated these projects, but the pamphlet did mention a nonprofit would appreciate donations. She made plenty of money, and why not choose a charity she could believe in? The thought this could be one more thing to help add to the healing gave her peace.

The rest of the day was spent browsing real estate sites and making plans to move. The level of joy and expectation surprised her. After eighteen months of surgery and rehab, this new chapter of her life was finally embraced wholeheartedly. The last thing to check off on her list was to attend that Kade Atwood concert with her friend Fawn. Seeing him in person, performing, might convince her she'd dodged a bullet.

On her final day, the foreman came strolling out of the barn. He reminded her of her dad and noticed the way Mozart ran to him.

"I understand my best friend was born here," she called to him.

He joined her, all smiles as he pushed his ball cap to the back of his head. "No kidding? Maybe that's why this guy is so friendly to me." Bobby Joe introduced himself and patted Mozart's head.

"I made a pitcher of sweet tea if you'd like to sit a spell, as they say around here."

"Sounds great. It's gonna be a hot one today," he informed her.

Vivian let him talk about the camp and how successful it had been for those in need. When she rubbed her prothesis, she realized she wore shorts for the first time. No one outside her medical team had seen her so exposed.

"Care if I ask what happened?" He leaned back in the rocker and eyed her carefully.

"Oh, the Taliban and I had a difference of opinion on how to get in a Black Hawk helicopter." She chuckled. "At least, it was just below the knee. Could have been worse." She held up her hand. "Still trying to get this to work right. Doctors said if I'm a good girl and do what I'm told, I might be able to do simple surgeries in the future."

"Best of luck to you, Colonel."

"Just call me Vivian. Anyway, how's the puppy you had to rescue?"

"Physically, pretty good, the vet said. Mentally, she seems a little sad and shy. The owner got really sick and couldn't take care of her. She's six months old, and there's a lot of development and trust that goes on during such a crucial time."

"Can I see her?"

"Sure. I'll bring her up in a bit to visit. I have a few chores then I'll be back. I might even convince you to take another dog. I'm not convinced I should send her to a veteran who is still adjusting when she hasn't had a good start."

"We'll see. I can't wait to meet her."

Vivian watched the foreman go about his chores before she returned the glasses to the sink and washed them. Today was her last day, and she wanted to get on the road before the forecasted storms moved back in. She planned to stop in Fort Campbell, Kentucky for the night at the home of a friend she met in medical school. Hopefully tomorrow, she'd hit the road again and make it to Fort Leonard Wood in Missouri.

"Colonel?" Vivian heard a tap at the screen door while she was packing up.

Mozart started prancing around and barking. "Calm down," she ordered. He immediately obeyed but whined up at her. She pushed him back and told him to stay as she went out onto the porch where the foreman held the six-month-old lab.

"She's kind of little, isn't she?" Vivian noticed as she scratched behind her ears.

"Yeah. She was the runt of the litter. If we sold them, she wouldn't have brought top dollar, but she still had a lot of potential. I'm afraid maybe she was left alone too much. Couldn't be helped. You never know when sickness will strike. The owner discovered he had cancer. He and his wife were barely coping and thought it best if she came back here."

The copper-colored pup had big expressive eyes that melted Vivian at first sight. Her tail wagged at her touch. "Can I hold her?"

The pup was gently handed off as Mozart continued to whine from the kitchen. She sat down in the rocking chair and tried to get acquainted. It didn't take long for the puppy to snuggle up and begin to doze.

"Can Mozart join us? I've been thinking about getting another dog because I'll be working long hours and hate for him to be alone."

The foreman slipped a leash on Mozart and led him out. A lot of tail wagging and sniffing ensued. When the copper puppy leaned toward him and began licking Mozart, Vivian knew she'd found another piece of life's puzzle.

"Is it even possible I can take her? I'm already in love."

"You already have one of our dogs. But since this one has had a rough start and may require more attention than a wounded warrior can do right now, I'd say let's give it a try—if, you're sure."

She kissed the dog's silky head and laughed. "I'm positive. I want to make a donation to your Dog Tag Fund as well. Whatever you want me to do."

Soon the papers were signed, and Vivian felt yet another burden had been lifted. "We'll take good care of her. Won't we, Mozart?" The dog answered with a bark and a vigorous tail wagging, followed by a hilarious dance of enthusiasm.

The foreman's cell phone buzzed. He read it then

started down the steps. "Looks like I need to pick up the boss. Can you stick around to meet him?"

Vivian scanned the dark clouds rolling in. "I'm not sure. I'm going to load up my car, do a quick cleaning, and maybe head out."

"I'll be back in a couple of hours, so think about it." Bobby Joe checked over the final papers one more time.

"Either way, thanks so much for this. I didn't know how much I could use this refreshing retreat. I'll keep you posted about my new family member."

He waved goodbye and headed out to his truck. Vivian waited until he drove off before she went inside. It didn't take long for the two dogs to cozy up together and nap on the kitchen floor as she prepared to leave. Distant thunder made her check the weather app on her phone and then tried to decide if she should take a chance on leaving if a storm was headed her way.

~ ~ ~ ~

Kade wore his cowboy hat and sunglasses through the airport. No one would pay him any attention since he dressed like a lot of other people here. Nashville was full of wannabe music stars. Having a bodyguard dressed almost as his twin gave a stay-away vibe. Big noisy places he had to walk through no longer held the same appeal they did before Afghanistan. He flew commercial most of the time, although he could afford private. At times, he wanted to be like everyone else. Such interactions with everyday people kept him grounded and offered a reminder of where he came from and who he was, or at least who he used to be.

As he walked out the doors, his phone dinged.

"General Morgan, what's the word?"

"Could be worse."

"That doesn't sound good." He saw his foreman's truck approaching. "The two planes are now on the ground in Uzbekistan. Everyone made it out, including Rasheed."

"That sounds like a good thing," Kade said as he waved to the foreman. His bodyguard opened the door for him to ride shotgun before he scooted into the back seat.

"Except Rasheed was shot."

"How bad?"

"I'm not sure, but they requested medical attention when they landed, and they're still there. The first plane is slotted to leave in a couple of hours. Medics suggested Rasheed stay behind, but I nixed it. The Taliban might find him. They figured out who he was, and all hell broke loose at the last minute. His family wasn't hurt only because he ran interference."

"And our guys? All okay?"

"Yes. I don't know how they got out, but they did. I'm anxious to hear the story. If Rasheed is stable enough to continue the trip, they'll leave shortly after the first plane. They will be flying into MidAmerica St. Louis Airport in a place called Mascoutah, Illinois. One of those hush-hush places, so you didn't hear it from me. Do you want to be there when they land?"

"Damn right, I do," he answered sternly. "Can I land a plane there and skip the airlines?"

"Yeah. I'll get you the information and get it cleared when I know the ETA."

"Thanks, General Morgan. This means a lot."

"No. Thank you, Kade. I may have had you all

wrong."

Kade continued to hold the phone tightly and stare out the windshield but really didn't see anything but the expression on Rasheed's face when the soldiers had placed the handcuffs on him that awful night.

"Everything okay?" the foreman asked.

"I sure hope so." Kade took a deep breath then let it out slowly.

"Good because I want you to meet this houseguest when we get back home. I think you're going to like the colonel."

"Ya know what? I think I want to be alone for a while," Kade said, leaning his head back and closing his eyes.

"Sure. Glad you're home, boss."

"Me too. Looks like a storm moving in. Hope it lasts until night. I sleep a whole lot better listening to the rain. If the colonel is still there, I'll just bunk with you, if that is okay."

Chapter 20

Kade watched from inside MidAmerica St. Louis Airport. Such a vast setup for no one to be there, especially since it was close to a metropolitan city. It basically sat in the middle of nowhere in a cornfield.

"I'm not going to even ask what goes on here, General Morgan."

"Good boy. Keep it that way. I don't even know. Well, at least the big picture. It does operate regular flights during the week." He chuckled then winked at him.

The plane had landed thirty minutes earlier, and the ground crew hustled securing the perimeter. The first plane had arrived five hours before at Scott Air Force Base, which was not far from here. Various kinds of scenarios began to work their way through Kade's imagination. He decided asking questions would not endear him to anyone, no matter how much money he threw at this mission.

"They're about to deplane, Kade. We can wait at the

gate. They politely requested we let them do a quick security scan on us before we can head that way." The general talked as he moved forward. He was right; it took only a few minutes and, given the way they greeted him, Kade had the definite impression this wasn't his first visit.

The Afghans filed off one by one. Some carried children; others had a small suitcase no bigger than a briefcase. These people arrived with little or nothing at all. Yet, this meant the world to them to be here. Several agency representatives waited to assist them to make the transition easier.

"What will happen to these people, General?" Kade watched a few desperate faces light up as they surveyed the huge interior of the airport, but just as quickly, stared back down at the floor as if protecting themselves.

"There are several communities in Illinois and Missouri waiting to help them get settled: schools, language classes for those who need it, places to live, and jobs. It's a complete package. The only family on hold is Rasheed's because of our understanding you arranged a similar organization to help his family."

"Yeah. My people should be here by morning, and we can decide how to progress. It's my hope he can get job training as a EMT or at least a related job. He expressed a desire to do work in the medical field, since that's what he did in Afghanistan."

Kade watched the families enter the airport, heads bowed, children clinging to their parents who shuffled along. Once they were approached by their helpers, their faces shone with hope. It touched him greatly.

"Where is Rasheed?" he asked General Morgan.

Then the man he hoped he could help emerged from

the jetway bridge, pushed in a wheelchair by one of the men sent to rescue him. A woman carrying a baby followed with three other children. Kade stepped forward. Rasheed twisted his neck to peer around people blocking his line of sight. It was difficult to let the ex-Marine gently move him forward.

"Rasheed!" Kade yelled at the same time the man pointed his way.

He pushed forward as the soldier helped him stand.

"Rasheed, welcome to America," Kade said surprised at his own relief to see the man.

Rasheed burst into tears, fell forward into Kade's arms, and hugged him tightly. "You did not forget me. You did not forget your promise." His body convulsed with relief and sobs. The rest of his family circled Kade and embraced the moment.

The overwhelming joy and thankfulness of these Afghans shook him to his core. General Morgan laid his hand on his shoulder. "It's okay, son, to be moved by this. You done good here. I'm proud of you."

"I hope Vivian is too," he said, blinking back emotion. "She meant everything to me."

"Wait, Kade, what are—"

"We need to move this along, General Morgan," the Marine interjected. "We have a schedule, and it's important we get these folks situated as soon as possible. They are tired and hungry. We also want to get this plane out of here."

General Morgan stole a sideways glance at Kade, who had already moved among the other Afghans as he pushed the wheelchair forward. Something was seriously off about what Kade knew concerning Vivian, or, in this case, didn't know. Addressing this problem could wait a little longer. For now, these people required his attention.

~ ~ ~ ~

Now that the wheels of safety had been set into motion, the general didn't have another free moment for Kade. His assistant showed up in St. Louis and helped with the transition of Rasheed's family to Tennessee. His team was already waiting to take the next steps. If further investigation was required, the FBI also would be standing by, along with various immigration personnel. The general still couldn't believe at how smoothly it went, considering it almost didn't happen a few days ago.

The part he needed to finish up was informing Vivian that Rasheed's family had been rescued. She had fretted over him for so many months, knowing to be left behind meant a certain death sentence he did not deserve. Should he tell her what Kade said at the airport? Was it possible that his absence in not showing up for Vivian was a misunderstanding?

"Bud, what great news," Vivian said excitedly. "Please, tell me the whole story. I'm so surprised. I know you must have had to keep this hush-hush and couldn't tell me, so this is so fantastic."

The general cleared his throat. "You need to know something else, Vivian." He cleared his throat. "If it hadn't been for Kade Atwood, it would never have happened. He financed the whole operation. Found the right people and made sure a lot of deserving Afghans got out of the danger zone. Many wouldn't have lasted but a few more weeks. Rasheed was shot but will make a full recovery. He is one happy guy." He could hear her sigh. "One more thing."

"What is it? How badly is Rasheed injured?"

"No. No. He'll be fine. It's about Kade." The general waited, but Vivian didn't respond. "Kade hoped this made you proud of him. He sounded genuinely sincere about that. Said you had meant a lot to him."

She chuckled lightly. "Well, sure I did. Thanks to our little romance, if that's what it was, he has another number-one best-selling album."

"Maybe he still cares."

"I'm sure the stand-up guy Kade Atwood is remembering me fondly. But let's face it, I am not the glamorous arm candy guys like him are used to having."

"Listen here, young lady, you are beautiful, a hero, and everything I ever wanted in a daughter. I feel blessed each day your parents made me and your aunt Ann your godparents. And I admit, I didn't like that country crooner taking a shine to you in Afghanistan because I thought he was just a rich boy who was full of himself."

"And you don't think that now?" Another laugh caught him off guard. "Don't get me wrong. What he did for Rasheed and the other Afghans was generous and amazing. But we both know it is just good for business and his reputation to do it."

"That's just it. No one knows he financed this, and he wants to keep it that way."

"Okay. So, you're a fan. Whatever his reason, I'm glad those poor people made it out. If he wants the credit—eventually, so be it. The important thing is they are safe. Thanks for letting me know. It has made my day. I love you, Ben. You and Aunt Ann plan on coming to visit when I get settled in Tennessee. Promise."

"Your aunt has already made plans to head that way. Talk to you soon."

~ ~ ~ ~

Vivian gazed out the large windows of their hotel room overlooking Busch Stadium. The Cardinals were in the ninth inning and winning. She'd always enjoyed going to the games with her dad and General Morgan when she was growing up. Her mom and Aunt Ann would go shopping and tried to get her to come, but she loved hearing her dad and the general talk farming and the military. Her mom and Aunt Ann were sisters and had married these guys when they were barely out of high school.

After losing both her parents, they had stepped in and become her guardians her senior year in high school. Without them, she may have given up on her dream of becoming a doctor. The general wasn't going to consider such a decision. Now, here she was, hanging on for dear life to continue the dream and be an exceptional physician if being a surgeon had become a faded dream.

Fawn, her dear friend from Arcadia Valley, had carried the Kade Atwood concert tickets around like they were the Holy Grail. She had joined her in Waynesville at Fort Leonard Wood for the night and together, they'd driven to St. Louis. The general surprised her with extra tickets for the concert and told her to have a lottery for anyone who wanted to go from her post. He would meet them at the hotel where her aunt Ann waited. The ten soldiers received their rooms free, along with a food allowance at a fancy steak house.

"General, how did you get these tickets?" Vivian had

asked suspiciously.

"I helped Kade on the Afghan rescue. His assistant sent this appreciation gift to do as I saw fit. Apparently, he does something like this at each city where he has a concert. Last month at Fort Campbell, he did a concert on base for free. It was a big hit. He took time to meet the families afterward." The general smiled mischievously.

"I'm not sure I'm buying that, but whatever. Can we sit together?"

"I managed to get us all in the same section after talking to his assistant about my family wanting to come." He kissed her on the forehead. "You are family. Besides, he doesn't know you'll be there, so don't let this spoil your good time. I want you to enjoy the show. I hear it's pretty good."

Vivian stroked his arm. "My guys needed this. Thanks for the tickets. They deploy next week, so this was a great idea." Now, she focused on the present since Fawn might drive her crazy.

"What time should we go?" Fawn asked, studying the tickets for the hundredth time. "I think the general said we're to be out front at six thirty for the party bus. I noticed a few of the privates and corporals were pretty cute. I might ditch you later, Vivian."

"And if you do, I'll tell Garrett Horton, who is head over heels in love with you. Are you ever going to tell me what went wrong between you two?"

"Yes. But not tonight. I want to enjoy the music, food, and those hunks in uniform." She hugged Vivian. "Surely, there is a good-looking officer out there, waiting in the wings for you."

"I'll keep an eye out for him." Vivian chuckled. "We

better get dressed. I understand we're supposed to wear our uniforms to get into the box seats."

Fawn checked herself in the mirror one more time. "It's been a long time since I went to the Fox Theater. I'll bet we have a butler tonight, since we have box seats."

"I have to admit, I'm a little excited. I haven't been to a concert in maybe four years, except on a military base. Most of the time, I had to work. There always seemed to be an emergency in the surgical unit to patch a wound or remove something. One crazy mishap after another." She buttoned up her jacket. "That's how I met Kade. He was all country charm and dreamy eyes."

Fawn wrapped both arms around her. "I'm sorry. This was a bad idea. I don't know what I was thinking."

"You didn't know until I told you. You already had the tickets, and who am I to rain on your parade." She hugged Fawn and pulled her shoulders back. "Let's do this, soldier!" she commanded, making her friend stand at attention and salute.

<h1 style="text-align:center">CHAPTER 21</h1>

Kade tuned his guitar while the other band members munched on snacks provided by the Fox Theater. The small talk remained quiet and relaxed. Each member had their own way to mentally prepare for the concert. This would be the last one on the tour. Entertainment gossip hinted he might be doing a tour in Europe next spring, but Kade and his band were tired. No one wanted to commit at the moment. Right now, he wanted to return to Tennessee and work on the resort project, write music, and go barefoot.

The idea of building his new house preoccupied his mind and he believed this would be therapeutic for him to make a plan. He'd purchased another fifty acres near the retreat area where he'd built the three-bedroom house. The barn was mostly used for the dog kennel. As the dream progressed, he also had been talking to physical therapists about getting a few therapy horses for amputees. He'd been convinced of the benefits and wanted to explore it a bit more. At least, this kept his mind occupied.

Rasheed's family had entered a new life in Lewisburg, Tennessee. He helped out at the VA clinic and was getting on-site training. The last he spoke to him, a few former soldiers, now firemen, had taken it upon themselves to train him in being a paramedic. He still needed to go to school, but at least he'd have a little experience and understand the lingo.

"It's time for the warm-up act, Mr. Atwood. They're going on stage now." It was the stage manager.

Kade gave him a thumbs-up. "Oh wait. Did General Morgan make it with his soldiers for the concert? I want to be sure to recognize them tonight."

"I'll double-check, sir."

Sixty minutes later, it was his turn. The introduction of the band came first then Kade walked out on stage, singing as he strummed his guitar. The crowd was on their feet with thunderous applause. He lost himself in the music and often invited the audience to sing along. He stopped several times to talk about his songs and how they came to be, without giving too much away. The news had covered him enough concerning Afghanistan when the camp had been overrun, but for the most part, his interaction had been suppressed.

Halfway through the concert, he stopped to honor all active and inactive military men and women. He also honored the Gold Star families who had lost a member because of their service. Finally, he honored his special guests in the box seats nearest the stage. He had them rise, and the whole audience gave a standing ovation.

"Thank you. Thank you. Thank you. And I want anyone here who is struggling or has someone in their family suffering from PTSD, please reach out to those who can help. You don't have to do this alone. When you leave, there will be counselors and other resources available to you. Please. Let them know how they can contact you and let's make this right."

He laid his hand on his heart and walked around the stage strumming his guitar. It was the beginning of "Whiskey and Sweet Tea." As the music played, he spoke into the microphone. "Many have asked where this song came from, and I have been reluctant to talk about it. I met an incredible woman when I was in Afghanistan. She inspired this song."

When Kade asked different military groups to stand, Vivian never expected the spotlight to be shined on her group. A wave of panic welled up inside her so that she wanted to run. General Morgan sat on one side of her and gently took her wounded hand that would always bear the scars of war. Even Fawn reached over to take her good hand and squeezed. It lasted a few seconds, and the lights went back down. Considering how bright the lights were pointing at the stage and flashes of fans snapping pictures, she felt confident Kade wouldn't see her. Then she realized the large screens on stage behind Kade exposed her. Chances of him seeing that later were not good, so she relaxed until he began talking about "Whiskey and Sweet Tea."

The big screen zeroed in on his face, especially his eyes that appeared to water as he sang. People sang the last chorus along with him. He closed out the concert with several more songs from his latest album before signing off. Before the second stage call, she told Fawn she'd wait in the lobby for her and the others. Her aunt Ann followed her out but knew enough not to ask any questions.

Back at the hotel, everyone went to dinner and topped the evening off enjoying a nightcap. Vivian loved being around the enlisted men and women who attended the concert. And, as expected, they couldn't say enough good things about Kade Atwood. The general and Aunt Ann joined them during dinner but turned in early.

"All in all, it wasn't so bad," Vivian admitted to Fawn the next morning. "I believe Kade is sincere in helping the military, and he certainly came through for Rasheed and his family. I told you about him, right?"

"Yes, you did. Do you plan to try and see Kade while you're here?"

"The general says he may live near Nashville. That's probably ninety minutes away if he lives near the airport so he can come and go quickly."

"Awkward. I mean—will this be hard on you?"

She zipped her bag shut. "I don't think so. Maybe. I don't know. I understand the brass blamed part of the camp being overrun because everyone lost focus on their job. Hard to say if the outcome would have been different if he hadn't been there. The truth was the Taliban wanted a female doctor, and that was me. I was kidnapped, but he volunteered to go too. It helped having a man with me in that culture."

Fawn lifted the bag off the bed. "He deserted you during your whole—rehab."

"I forgave him a long time ago. Besides, I have a lot to do when I take this job. Chances of us running into each other will be few and far between if ever. As I said, it's a long way from Lewisburg. It's all pretty rural. He tours most of the year, I think. I have no intentions of reaching out. Talk about awkward."

"I can't believe you're leaving in a few days. I wanted

to go with you, but school begins, and I have to be there."

"Those kindergarteners are going to love you, Fawn. I'll be fine. I don't have much anyway. I'm renting a place near the clinic until I find something more permanent."

"Come and have Thanksgiving with my folks. My mother will be ecstatic."

"No promises, but I'll put it on the calendar."

~ ~ ~ ~

Kade sat at the kitchen table of the little house he'd built to feel closer to Vivian. He thought she would have loved it, front porch and all. He opened his computer to go over the promo shots of his last two concerts, one of them in St. Louis where General Morgan had brought his people. He had hoped he'd get a chance to talk to him and bring his group backstage, but his manager had arranged for groups of fans who paid extra to come backstage and meet him. Several were city officials and congressmen. It grew late by the time that was wrapped up. If he didn't get enough rest, the nightmares would return. Sleeping in the next morning also caused him to miss the general. Only one more concert before he could go home.

"Morning, Kade. You got in late last night." The foreman stood in the doorway wiping his feet on the rug. "I see you're already hard at it. Guess you'll be home for a while. I contacted the architect last week and made an appointment for you tomorrow."

"Did you mention I want a recording studio? I'm kind of done going into Nashville for that. At this point, I want to stay home more."

"I know you do, but be careful you don't shut yourself

completely off from the world." The foreman's voice deepened, and his forehead creased.

"Not much chance of that. Anyway," he said, scrolling through the pictures from the St. Louis concert. He backed up the pictures and zeroed in on the seats he'd secured for the general. The general stood straight and tall, holding the hand of Major Vivian Palmer. He jumped up from his chair, flipping it over. "You lying sack of…"

The foreman came around and leaned down to stare at the screen. "What?"

"Her. She's the one I told you about who I fell hard for in Afghanistan. I thought she was dead."

The foreman used his fingers to widen the screen. "Kade, she was here. I mean here, in this house."

"What are you talking about?" Kade was skeptical about what he was looking at.

"Remember I told you a colonel had rented this house? That's her." He flipped back through the guest records in his notebook. "Yeah. Colonel Vivian Palmer."

"Not Major Palmer?" he asked, still a little bewildered. "I guess she could have been promoted. It stands to reason after all the work she'd done in such a war zone. And she stayed here?"

"Yeah. Brought her dog, which it turns out, was one of our puppies. She took the pup I rescued while she was here as well. They left the day I picked you up at the airport. Remember, I wanted you to meet the colonel."

Kade ran his hands through his hair then began to pace. "She's alive. All this time I thought she was gone forever. Was she okay?"

The foreman paused. "Well, she did have a prothesis. The lower part of one leg was missing and something wasn't right about one hand. I don't remember which one. Said she was an out-of-commission surgeon working toward getting back in the game. I only noticed the leg because she had shorts on. You didn't know about that either?"

"Hell no," he growled. "And the entire time, I thought the general was being on the up-and-up with me. He wanted her for himself. No wonder he never mentioned her. The message I got…" Taking a deep breath, he grabbed his ball cap and headed out the door. "I'm going for a walk. We can talk later. I don't trust myself with any business decisions right now."

The tree-lined trails zigzagging around the property opened up to parallel green pastures then gardens to give a calming effect. Split-rail fencing was set back from the wide path to keep the cattle away from the guests. In the distance, a rooster crowed and hickory branches rubbing against each other rattled. A few hawks flew from the top of a white pine as he continued to storm around the property, trying to piece together the lies he'd been fed for almost two years.

Finally, he stopped at a wooden bridge to peer down into the clear creek water the children found great for wading when veteran families visited. At times, their voices carried on the wind to where he sat on the front porch. Although his heart was pumping hard and sweat caused him to remove his cap to wipe his brow, his brain slowed enough to try and deal with the idea Vivian might still be alive. To know she had been here, sitting on the front porch, drinking iced tea, brought a wave of emotion that nearly overwhelmed him. To top it off, she now owned his dogs and had attended his concert with the man who'd betrayed him.

Why hadn't she reached out to him? Did she blame him for the horrible things that happened to her? Clearly, her life had been radically altered, unlike his. Maybe he reminded her of how much danger they'd been in or that he could have done more to protect her from the Taliban. They were the ones who took away her ability to be a surgeon. How could he possibly expect her to love or even care for him the same way he still loved her.

The other matter was General Morgan. If he had been honest with him, he and Vivian could have moved forward and tried to work things out between them. He pulled his phone from his shirt pocket and dialed the last number he had for the general.

"General Morgan's office," came a no-nonsense male voice.

"I'd like to speak to the general ASAP."

"I'm sorry. He is unavailable right now. May I take a message?"

"Yes, you may. Tell the general Kade Atwood is on the line, and he'd better pick up, or I'm going to make his life a living hell."

CHAPTER 22

The general pulled his shoulders back and waved his secretary off when he entered to let him know a disgruntled Kade Atwood was on the phone.

"He's mad as a hornet, sir. Want me to tell him you'll call him back?"

"No. Put it through. I'll take care of it. I've been meaning to talk to him concerning a few things anyway. Don't worry. I'll handle it. Thanks," the general said as he put his hand on the black phone on the desk. He decided he preferred these kinds of phones over the cell. The speaker activated as he hit receive.

"Kade, I hear you have a bee in your bonnet. What's up?"

"What's up is you've been lying to me about Vivian. You told me she died, and now I see a picture of you holding her hand at my concert in St. Louis. Pretty convenient you pushing me out of the picture so you could have her all to yourself."

"Hold on. It's not what you think. Besides, I never told you she was dead. As a matter of fact, I didn't tell you anything except the outcome of her surgery was not what we hoped, but she would be fine. There would be a lot of hurdles but Vivian was tough."

"I received a different message implying she'd died and you were sorry. Whoever you sent to deliver that message, it came out completely different," he fumed.

"That would explain why you never came looking for her or why you kept talking about her in the past tense."

"Damn right," he huffed. "And you being with her in St. Louis? What about that?"

"My wife and I are Vivian's godparents. We stepped in when her dad died then my wife's sister. We don't have any children, so Vivian means the world to us. Yes, I held her hand when you flashed that damn light around the theater. Did anyone ever tell you it wasn't a good idea to do that around a bunch of military people who may have PTSD? Seeing you for the first time and being asked to stand up gave her a panic attack. She didn't want to come to the concert in the first place because she thinks you abandoned her."

"I love her. Why would she think such a thing?"

"She is not the woman you once knew. She's missing part of a leg, and her hand may never be able to do surgery again. For some crazy reason, she has the notion you wouldn't want an incomplete package. You being MIA all this time pretty much convinced her."

When Kade spoke, after a long silence, he'd calmed down. "I'm sorry, sir. I came unglued when I saw pictures the promotional people sent me this morning. I don't usually look at those, but this time, I was searching for you. We didn't get to talk while you were there, and I wanted to send you a few copies of the pictures."

"Kade, I'm sorry too. This is a total screwup in

communication. Those last few months in Afghanistan were a nightmare, as you can imagine. I was recovering from my wounds while trying to get our people out before a total collapse. I sent you a message. It's possible—"

"It most definitely happened, General Morgan."

"Yes. I should have followed up, but… My primary concern was Vivian and her well-being. It has not been easy. She's in a good place right now and has worked hard to pull herself together and move on. I worried your concert might set her back, but, like a good soldier, she carried on and is back at work."

"I need to find her, sir. I want to explain. I seriously thought I'd lost her forever. I don't care about her leg or her hand. I only want to be there for her. She is the bravest and most beautiful woman I've ever known."

"I'll let her know what happened. Then I'll get back to you. I know as soon as I hang up, you're going to put your bloodhounds on her location and may even find her. But I'm telling you to not, I repeat, do not go see her without me telling her how I screwed this up. Are you going to be okay if she still doesn't want to see you?"

"No. I'm going to see her with or without your permission. But I will wait a couple of days for it to sink in for her. I'm a little shell-shocked right now too. I'm angry and hurt at the same time. I'm sick to think I let her down."

"My wife is with her now. I'm going to join them for a few days. I want to be there in person when I tell her. Can I give her this number to call?"

"I'll be waiting for the call, sir. Thank you. I apologize for blowing up at you. I—"

"I get it. Betrayal is a hard thing to accept. I'm glad

we both have the truth now. Expect word from me in a few days or maybe even from Vivian."

"Thanks, General Morgan."

~ ~ ~ ~

Omar had finally received word from his contacts in Afghanistan that it was time to show his loyalty to the Taliban and his country, his true country, not the United States. He had come here as a student in 2018. It didn't take long for the long arm of the Taliban to reach out to him and enlist him as a possible soldier for the cause. It could be tomorrow or ten years from now, but the time would come to take action.

Now that he was a computer programmer and tech support for a large health care system, it didn't take long for the Taliban to, once again, enlist him to prove his worth. Part of him wanted no part of anything that could jeopardize his comfortable life. Now, he was married with a baby on the way, had made friends, and was well respected at his job. But there remained a shadow of doubt wherever he went, as if he might be dangerous because of his background. The idea he'd been passed over for several promotions began to eat away at his contentment.

He had no desire to return home because most of his family had disappeared or died. The Taliban was quick to remind him it was the foreign occupiers who destroyed his life. After watching the withdrawal of the troops in Afghanistan and the death of so many innocent people trying to leave, he began to wonder if it had been worth it? The blatant abandonment of those who had served the occupiers were left to fend for themselves in spite of having promised to protect them.

Omar reread the message he'd received days earlier. You must find the traitor Rasheed Nawabi who left our land in recent months. His whereabouts are unknown. He had medical training and friends in high places, along with a man named Kade Atwood. Because of this man, an army doctor we know as Major Palmer, and a General Morgan, many of our peaceful people lost their lives after welcoming them into our homes. It was a trap we did not see coming. You must seek vengeance on them.

The following days, he began a search for the soldiers mentioned. Kade Atwood was everywhere online, TV, and radio. Omar listened to his music and wondered why he'd won so many awards. Maybe the music glorified the self-serving lives of a materialistic world. Major Palmer and General Morgan were not as easy to locate, given the protection parameters officers followed after returning home. They all knew they could still be targets and continued their security training on a day-to-day basis. Americans thought of any and all scenarios, but they would fall back into the rhythm of living in the land of the free and home of the brave.

It wasn't until Omar watched a newsreel about different volunteer groups slipping into Afghanistan to rescue people, that he finally had a thread he could follow to find Major Palmer, now a colonel, and General Morgan. Although it took determination and using a lot of back doors to various unauthorized sites, he managed to find them. For the first time in over a year, he felt a sense of accomplishment. Now, what to do about it?

~ ~ ~ ~

Vivian finished her shift at the VA clinic and was told a visitor waited in her office to see her. Apparently, he had been wanting to touch base for several months. According to her boss, Mac, he had also served in Afghanistan and wanted to surprise her. She expected one of the soldiers she knew from there or maybe a former patient who managed to be one of her success stories.

"Why the secrecy, Mac? I don't like surprises, or have you forgotten?" Vivian allowed one of the nurses to cover her eyes with a bandana. Th doctor guided her to her office.

"I know. But you'll like this one. I promise. You've been working so hard here for the last two weeks, and I refuse to let the secret out of the bag. I promised the general."

Vivian huffed. "I bet my aunt doesn't know about this. She'd be down here with a buggy whip smacking you around if she knew you did this to me."

"Nope. The general kept her out of the loop too because he said she couldn't keep a secret, especially from you."

"Okay. Let's get this over with." She stretched her good hand out to touch the doorframe as the doctor pulled her into her office.

"You can remove your bandana now," the doctor announced.

Vivian pulled it down around her neck and blinked at the shadowy figure standing before her. A man came into focus as she blinked away the darkness.

"Good to see you, Colonel Palmer. Do you remember me?" he asked in choppy English.

Vivian sucked in her breath as tears pooled in her

eyes. "Rasheed!" she gasped. She stepped toward him with an outstretched hand to try and touch his arm. Before she could, he took it gently and kissed it then held it up to his face. "I am so glad to see you."

"May I hug you, Colonel Palmer?" he said shyly.

Without hesitation, Vivian stepped closer and pulled him into her arms. "Oh, Rasheed, I worried about you all those months. I'm sorry it took so long to bring you to the States."

"It would not have happened if it had not been for Mr. Atwood and General Morgan. It was mere hours before the Taliban would find and kill me and my family."

"I will leave you two to visit," Mac said, stepping into the hall. "My nurse will be right outside at the desk if you need her."

Vivian understood it might not be appropriate for him to be left alone with an unmarried woman, so she moved closer to the open door as he pulled up two chairs. "Please, Rasheed. Tell me everything. I want to know about your family, your work, your life. Can I get you tea?"

He grinned sheepishly. "I have developed a taste for your Southern sweet tea. Do you have any here?"

"If not, I'll make some." She couldn't believe how happy she felt, seeing her old friend. "I want you to start at the beginning."

CHAPTER 23

Omar watched the comings and goings of the trucks that turned into the Let It Roll Camp operated and owned by a wealthy country music personality who he knew to be Kade Atwood. The news of his work with veterans was beginning to leak out, although he didn't advertise his generosity, but military and veterans' groups sang his praises enough to catch the ear of the president. There was talk of the Presidential Medal of Freedom for all the work he did to help military families. The disgruntled Afghan listened with a certain amount of apathy to the testimonials and wondered who would hear the struggles of his people.

He spotted the country music star in the small town of Chapel Hill, talking to a few people at a local grocery store and again at the car wash where he had his truck detailed. There was no particular pattern to his comings and goings. A guard house at the entrance of the camp, where guests checked in, helped him decide to rule out driving through the gates without being noticed or detained.

The weakest link turned out to be General Morgan.

Since the general remained on active duty, a pattern quickly appeared so that Omar knew where he headed most of the time. The other weak link was his wife, Ann. Tracing her history, family, and whereabouts led her to Colonel Palmer. The obstacle had been thinking she was still a major. Connecting her to the general and his wife made his process much easier. The VA clinic where she worked might possibly have all the players in one place in the future.

His next stop was the VA clinic in Lewisburg, just a twenty-minute drive from the Let It Roll Camp. Spending a few days in the area gave him an idea of the heaviest traffic days and the number of staff. Only once did he spot Colonel Palmer who, as expected, was as vigilant of her surroundings as if she were walking the streets of Kabul on a dark night. Many of the veterans who entered the building did the same security scan, which included the rooftops, cars in the parking lot, and others walking to and from the building. Those vets were the ones he needed to watch. They probably wore a weapon and could drop a threat with one shot to the head. Although veterans needed medical care in one form or another, they were still in soldier mode, even the old ones. This, he didn't understand.

~ ~ ~ ~

The small two-bedroom house Vivian rented was freshly painted inside and out. The fenced backyard was perfect for the dogs. The hardwood floors were scuffed and faded to different shades of brown, depending on if the sun flooded through one of the many windows surrounding the house.

"Aunt Ann, you have done a wonderful job." Vivian hugged her aunt who beamed at the praise and accepted a kiss on the cheek. "I saw so many empty boxes on the front porch."

"Well, you didn't have a lot of things to bring. But I did line your kitchen shelves and put a shine on the pieces of furniture you brought with you. I think we should go shopping." Her aunt handed her a class of iced tea.

"I know. But I'm hoping to buy my own place first so I'll know exactly what I'll need. Besides, I have to save money too. Those dogs eat me out of house and home." She laughed. The dogs raised their heads as if they understood she was talking about them and wagged their tails.

"Come on. Let me give you the tour of what I did today. The general will be here soon, and I made his favorite dinner."

Vivian toured the bedrooms and checked out the bathroom. Her aunt lived for these kinds of projects to let her decorating talents shine. "Aunt Ann, do you have any idea what Bud wants to talk to me about? Said it would have to wait until he got here. He sounded serious. He's not sick, is he? I mean, he took a pretty good hit in Afghanistan and, although he recovered without any severe aftercare, he isn't getting any younger."

Ann laughed then winked at her. "I'll not tell him you said that. He's an old warhorse, and you know it. I have no idea, but he recently had a checkup and passed with flying colors. Must be about the military or medical units being deployed to different areas of the country and abroad. That last rescue mission worried him like a picnic fly. I put my foot down and said no more of that.

Let the younger men do dangerous stunts, along with those government fools who are clueless."

Vivian teared up sharing the story about her meeting with Rasheed and how much it meant to her. "He's been through so much, Aunt Ann."

"So have you, sweetheart." She hugged Vivian then pointed to a car pulling into the driveway. "That will be the general. I've missed him. Let's go give him a hard time."

"I'm all for that."

The dinner of barbequed ribs, grilled potatoes, and a fresh lettuce salad followed by coconut cake made everyone yawn and rub their stomachs. Vivian loved how her aunt always made the most delicious meals to feed them. The sun began to set, and a cool breeze toyed with the sheers as it pushed through the screen door and windows. She loved having things open so she could smell the earth and hear the birds.

"Let's get this cleaned up," the general said as he loaded the dishwasher. "I got a few things to talk to you ladies about. Mostly it's for Vivian, but, Ann, you need to hear this too."

Vivian cast a worried glance at her aunt whose brow creased in that concerned way she used to do when the general announced he would be deployed one more time. "Bud, you go sit down with Aunt Ann. The two of you have had a long day, and I can do this. Besides, we ate on paper plates. Not much to do. You guys should visit a bit."

She made a pot of coffee after wiping down the table and counters. Filling three cups, she suggested they move to the back porch and listen to the locusts so the dogs could burn off their energy.

The three remained quiet as they sipped their coffee and watched the dogs chase a territorial squirrel who apparently had a death wish. Several times, they chuckled at the antics but, finally, the general took a deep breath, signaling it was time to talk serious business.

"Vivian, I want to talk to you about Kade Atwood." The general leveled a fatherly glare at her, his brow wrinkled in concern.

"I don't really want to do that, Bud."

"Well, I'm gonna anyway, and I expect you to listen."

Vivian rolled her eyes, held her cup to her lips, and stared out into the darkness. "I'm listening."

"The first thing I want to tell you is that you need to stop hating Kade."

"I never said I hated him, Bud. I…"

"Loved him?" he asked. "Because he's crazy about you. The whole rescue of Rasheed was for you. He knew you promised him a way out, and he wanted to fulfill that promise."

"Good for him. He did me proud, I guess," Vivian said sarcastically.

"That place you stayed when you came down here, Let it Roll Camp? That belongs to him. He built it for veterans. Those dogs you are so crazy about were his puppies."

Vivian stared at him in disbelief. "What? Has he put a spell on you? I thought you disliked him. You kept telling me I could do better."

"Now, I'm thinking maybe he could do better," he insisted.

"Bud!" snapped Aunt Ann. "What is wrong with you?"

"Gee, thanks, Bud," Vivian growled. "What changed?

He charmed you like he does everyone else?"

The general handed her the letter he'd been carrying around for way too long. "He gave this letter for me to give you when he left Afghanistan. I shoved it into my gear to give you when I made it to Germany, which, as you know, took a couple of months. By that time, I'd forgotten about it. Well, my secretary found it and I thought I should still try and give it to you. I should be given some credit for not opening it and making sure I approved."

Vivian took the letter and ran her fingers over it. "My money is on you steamed it open and read it," she said suspiciously.

"Maybe I did, smarty pants. But the reason he didn't come around was because he thought you died from your injuries," he said hurriedly. "I sent a message to him after your surgery saying it was bad news and not what he hoped. Oh, there was more to the message, but he only got the bad news and sorry. Just so you know, he's messed up over it. He didn't know you were alive until he found pictures the other day from the St. Louis concert and saw you with me. Believe me when I say, I got an earful."

Vivian laid the letter in her lap then reached for her cup. "Does he know about my leg, my hand?"

"He does now. And you know what? He doesn't care. I made him promise not to try and contact you before I had a chance to explain. Little did I know until yesterday that Let It Roll was right down the road in Chapel Hill. The place was built in your honor. He literally thought you were dead, Vivian. Right now, he is confused, hurt, and anxious to see you, and that's besides being pretty pissed off at me. He never meant to abandon you."

Vivian opened her mouth to protest, but nothing came out. She was dumbfounded. "I don't want to see him and be hurt all over again when he realizes I'm not the woman I was in Afghanistan. I couldn't take that. Does he know I live so close?"

"I never told him. I promised to call him after I talked to you. I'm sure he has his bloodhounds out trying to find where you are. He is one determined country boy, Vivian. And I like him. A lot!"

Aunt Ann reached over and touched his arm. "Bud, she needs to process this. It's her decision."

"I know that." He snorted impatiently. "But he deserves to be heard. If it doesn't work out, then fine. Maybe you can work together to help the vets and military families. He's doing a hell of a job right now." The general started rocking in his chair. "I'd be proud to have him in our family," he said proudly.

"Oh. My. Gosh!" Vivian said in exasperation. "That's a first. Every guy who ever came around, you acted like you had a firing squad in the back room waiting for them to make one misstep."

"What's your point?" he asked matter-of-factly.

Both Vivian and her aunt chuckled at his comment.

"Do you have his number? I better get it over with before I lose my nerve." Vivian got to her feet. "I'll read the letter first."

"You don't have to decide tonight, sweetheart," Aunt Ann said as she gathered Vivian in her arms.

"And you listen to me, young lady. You are twice the woman and soldier of anyone I've ever met. Besides your aunt, you're the prettiest woman I know, and a fine doctor."

"Spoken like a real special dad, Bud. And I love you

like you were my dad. I hope you know that."

He rocked faster and pretended to focus on something in the dark. "Yeah. Yeah. Sweet talk. Just like your aunt does to manage me."

Vivian leaned down and kissed him on the cheek. "Give me your phone. Then he won't have my number." He pulled out his phone and scrolled down to the number before handing it to her. "Ann, why don't we go inside. I could use another piece of that coconut cake. Got any ice cream?"

Ann stood and pulled him up out of the rocker. "We'll go in, but you won't be getting any more cake tonight."

He slipped an arm around his wife and winked at Vivian. "She's kidding."

Vivian waited until they were out of earshot and sat back down in the rocker. There was enough light coming from the kitchen windows that reading the letter wasn't a problem. Taking a deep breath, she began to read. Tears welled up in her eyes as she could almost hear him telling her how much she made a difference in his life and how proud he was of her. No matter how things turned out with her surgeries and recovery, he would be there every step of the way.

She held the phone tightly in her hand. She had worked with the wounded, performed surgeries under impossible conditions, survived being kidnapped by the Taliban, and lost a leg in the process. None of it fazed her. So, why did this phone call scare her?

CHAPTER 24

Kade sat on the front porch swing with one leg propped up and the other touching the floor. A hoot owl let out its soft call and somewhere he heard the flapping of wings. He turned General Morgan's story over in his head constantly. Vivian alive. How could he have not followed up on finding out what her last hours were like? The reason was he didn't want to hear it. The idea she'd suffered and died senselessly after all she'd done to make life better for those soldiers, ripped a hole inside him. The emptiness engulfed him like a tsunami. Music was the only thing that brought her memory to him each day. He didn't even have a picture of her.

And now, he waited. Would she forgive him? Why would she? He'd abandoned her when she needed him the most.

His cell phone rang from inside the house. Rushing inside, he grabbed up the phone and saw that it was General Morgan. "Hello—" The line disconnected immediately. Taking a deep breath, he counted to ten

191

then twenty and, finally, to thirty. As he was about to redial, the phone rang again.

"General Morgan, sir. I couldn't get to the phone in time. I apologize. Did you talk to Vivian? I have been pacing the floor ever since you told me she was alive. Is she okay? Did you explain? Can I see her?"

"Kade?" Vivian spoke softly. "It's me."

Kade stepped back out on the porch and returned to the swing. "V-Vivian," he stuttered. "Vivian, I-I can't believe it's you." She didn't respond. "Please. Can I come see you? I'll leave tonight, if you'll just tell me where you are."

A soft laugh came through to him. He recognized the sound and remembered how it felt to hold her in his arms in that faraway land. "Kade, Afghanistan affects people in different ways. We were caught in a difficult situation and—"

"No. I loved you from that first day. And I know you grew to care for me."

"I've never met anyone like you. But, Kade, I have a long road ahead of me. You deserve better. I won't be doing the Texas two-step for a while."

"I'm not much of a dancer anyway." He reached for the whiskey bottle he'd been nursing then set it down, knowing he didn't have to escape one more day. "Vivian, where are you? Let's see each other and decide how we want to move forward. No pressure."

"I'm about twenty minutes from you. I moved to Lewisburg to work at the VA clinic. I wanted a fresh start. I'm still in the military as a reservist. I thought I could still serve for a while then maybe go into private practice."

"Lewisburg?" He ran his fingers through his hair.

"You've been this close and I didn't even know? I kept meaning to go talk to Dr. Mac and well, I guess I was just tired of pretending I was okay with you being gone. I let you down. I'm so sorry, Vivian."

"Not your fault. I had a lot of recovering to do. I actually saw Rasheed today. It was a wonderful thing you did for all those people. Look, I need to go. This is all too much to comprehend right now."

"Please, let's talk for a while. Or I can hop in the truck and be there in no time."

"Let's wait until tomorrow to meet. But I'm willing to talk a little longer—if that's what you want."

~ ~ ~ ~

Omar had watched the coming and goings of Colonel Vivian Palmer for several days. When he saw the man Rasheed enter the VA clinic, he made a few inquiries and found out he worked nearby. His contact at the airlines alerted him that General Morgan had also arrived to visit Colonel Palmer.

He shaved his beard, bought a Tennessee Titans cap, and dressed like a good ole boy to fit in with the locals. Because like most Afghans, his skin fair and his eyes light colored, no one paid him any attention. Driving to the VA clinic with a few necessary supplies, he parked his rented truck and walked inside as he checked his watch. He hoped the parking lot would fill up before he activated the explosive device. Taking out a knife, he ripped his jeans and shirt sleeve before running the blade down his skin. Inhaling deeply, Omar walked inside.

~ ~ ~ ~

"You're going to brush your hair completely out if you don't stop." Aunt Ann peeked into Vivian's bedroom and shook her finger. "You're pretty as a peach. He's just a man. Well, a darn good-lookin' man, but still, he gets in his pants the same as all the others. Now, if you ask me—"

"Aunt Ann." Vivian applied a little lipstick and mascara and gave herself a final appraisal in the mirror. Blue jeans, a scoop-necked T-shirt, and tennis shoes. "I'm just going to be me," she said, glancing toward her aunt. "If he doesn't like it, he can lump it."

"That's the spirit. Now go help the general with those pancakes."

Vivian pushed her food around her plate but managed to carry on a conversation as if nothing was unusual about the day. Kade wouldn't arrive until eleven, so there was plenty of time to pretend she was fine. When she took her coffee on the back porch to watch the dogs begin their daily recon of destroying the squirrel who taunted them, she made a mental list of the questions she planned to ask Kade.

Last night had been a lot easier than she thought possible. They fell into the rhythm of small talk and didn't venture toward personal matters or the past. Even if this didn't work out, she knew Kade would be her friend, and their desire to help military families was a project both wanted to continue.

Aunt Ann came out onto the porch. "Vivian, Dr. Mac called. I answered your phone. Better get back to him. Said it was important."

She came inside and dialed him, concerned he'd

reached out on her day off. She worked every other Saturday if they had appointments. There were none today. "Mac, what's up?"

"We have a situation here. A good ole boy who says he wants only the new doctor to stitch him up. Looks like he should have gone to the ER, but he's a vet, or so he claims. I'm trying to pull up information on him since Joany hasn't come in yet. He's our first patient. Says he doesn't trust the regular medical folks, and his friend Rasheed recommended you. He's bleeding like a stuck hog and won't let anyone help him but you."

"Of course. I'll be there in a few minutes. I'll go ahead and contact the paramedics to meet me there. Maybe Rasheed could help too. I'll leave him a message."

"Thanks, Vivian. Oh, I think Joany just arrived."

Vivian clicked off and headed to her room, the general at her heels. "Bud, I've got to run to work. A guy is hurt and only wants me to take care of him."

"Have you met him before?" he asked suspiciously.

"I don't think so. Guess he knows Rasheed, and he recommended me. Anyway, he's causing a ruckus and won't let anyone touch him but me. He may need stitches. At least I can do that—I think."

"I don't like it. I'll go with you. I'll tell Ann we're slipping out for a bit."

"What if Kade gets here before I return? You should stay."

"I'll call him to meet us there."

Vivian huffed and rolled her eyes. "Well, that would be romantic. Blood. Chaos. You. Me. Just like old times. With any luck, I'll have blood splatter on me, too. I've handled worse. Ann has missed you. Stay here. I shouldn't be long. How bad could it be?" She shoved her phone in her purse and headed to the door. "Watch the dogs, will you? They need fresh water."

"You call me when you get there and tell me things are okay."

Vivian hugged his neck. "Yes, sir!"

"I mean it, Vivian." The general walked her to her car. "You hear about some of these guys slipping off the edge all the time. It's not like taking care of a wounded soldier in Afghanistan where you hold their life in your hands and they are so grateful, maybe a little in love with you."

"The only patient I ever had who maybe fell for my bedside manner was Kade Atwood. And we know how that turned out." Her laugh drew a smile on an otherwise sour expression. "I'll call you. Promise."

~ ~ ~ ~

Kade pulled into the driveway and exited the car slowly. He eyed the surroundings, realizing the little house with the front porch was exactly where he'd pictured her sitting. Last night, she said she also had a back porch so she could watch her dogs run and play. Hearing her voice for almost two hours went a long way at healing his shattered heart. Knowing that any second he'd be able to see her gave him the jitters.

He went around to the other side of his truck and pulled out a bouquet of flowers and shoved a small velvet box in his vest pocket. No way was he going to let her go again.

A trim lady with brown hair streaked with gray answered the door before he could knock.

She pushed the screen door open and eyed him mischievously. "Well, if it isn't the devil in blue jeans himself," she said, putting her hands on her hips. "If you're lookin' for my niece, she left."

Kade's heart sank as he lowered the bouquet of wild flowers. "Oh," was the only thing he could manage to say.

General Morgan pushed past her and stuck out his hand. "She's yanking your chain, Kade. Vivian was called in to work for an emergency. Said she shouldn't be long. She promised to call me when she got there. Guess I'm going to have to demote her. She's gotten a little too big for her britches since she became a colonel. Next thing you know, she'll try to tell me what to do."

Aunt Ann slapped him on the upper arm. "I already do that. One more female bossing you around sounds about right to me." She winked at Kade. "Sorry. I'm Ann. Nice to meet you."

"These are for you, Ms. Ann." He handed her the flowers.

"Why those are lovely. I'll get a vase. You boys come in here and talk so I can hear you."

General Morgan checked his phone again. "I don't understand why she didn't call me back." He told Kade why she went into work. "I didn't like it, but I let her talk me out of going with her. She wanted me here when you came. I'm giving it another few minutes. She doesn't answer."

"Someone is turning into the driveway. Maybe that's her." Kade shaded his eyes.

The man hoped out and ran up to the porch.

"Rasheed?" Kade asked with a smile. "What are you doing here? Come for the reunion?" It was then he noticed the look of terror in his eyes as he panted. "What's wrong?"

The general frowned as he tried to reach Vivian one more time. "I tried to contact the fire station and left a message for Rasheed earlier."

"Yes, sir. I got it. That's why I am here. I tried the clinic too. Just a busy signal. Colonel Palmer is in danger. I think someone is waiting to kill her at the clinic. Please, we must hurry."

Vivian parked in her space and carefully made her way to the front door. It was one of those days when her prothesis leg wanted to rebel. Today, she had a slight limp. Maybe it was because she sat too long last night in the late-night air talking to Kade. She had not allowed herself to admit how much she'd missed hearing his voice. The morning walk she missed today must have had more benefits than she believed. Maybe when she got back home, Kade wouldn't mind taking one. She took a deep breath. That felt good to believe such a thing might be possible.

When Vivian pulled on the locked door, a little voice in her head started screaming to be careful. Running her hand down the side of her denim purse, she felt the small caliber weapon she always carried. Her eyes darted to the rooftop. Nothing. The parking lot. Only four vehicles: hers, a late-model truck, and two vehicles belonging to Mac and Joany. No movement inside.

She could tap on the door, alerting whoever was inside that she'd arrived. After all, her presence had been requested. Backing up to disappear from view of the glass front door, she pulled her phone from the front zipper pocket. The battery was too low for her to contact the general. It reminded her how she'd neglected to put it on the charger the night before. Kade mesmerized her more than she thought. At least she could still call 911 emergency. She pushed the button.

The connection cut out several times while she tried to tell the dispatch there may be a medical emergency at the clinic with an unruly patient. Keeping her voice low, she managed to add she'd been locked out after being summoned. The line finally went dead. Lesson learned. Always remember to be prepared.

Slipping the phone into her pants pocket, she removed the Glock 43X. She'd only recently purchased it and had managed to take it to a gun range nearby. She felt comfortable enough to use it now. Mac had told her he kept a gun locked in a safe inside the clinic in case a situation should ever arise. He'd given her the code in case she ever sensed trouble. Although this was unnerving, Mac assured her that not once had there been a problem. Most of the grumbling came from Korean and Vietnam vets, not the new guys. The older ones were easily pacified with letting them talk about their aches and pains, and a story about where they served.

She dropped her purse behind one of the decorative bushes lining the sidewalk that wound to the side door. There were windows here where you could see into the lobby up front and down the hall to the examining rooms. The blinds were shut, cutting off any possibility of discovering what might be going on. Moving down the sidewalk toward the rear of the clinic, she discovered the back door ajar and unlocked. Although the blinds were partially closed, the windows back here were cracked enough she could scope out the inside.

Dr. Mac and Joany sat on the floor. Mac was a short man but wiry and worked out every day. For him to be sporting a black eye and blood dripping from his hairline told her the man holding a gun on them must have caught them off guard. Joany was crying and leaning into Dr. Mac who had his arm around her.

The man's profile did not tell her much, except he looked like anyone else in the area. He held his gun in one hand and his phone in the other. But then his phone rang and he quickly answered it and began speaking in Pashto; the language of Afghanistan. With a lot of head bobbing and shouting, he turned his back on the door where she waited. He failed to notice when Vivian slipped inside. When he clicked off, he turned around to find Colonel Vivian Palmer pointing her weapon at him.

"Drop the gun," she ordered in Pashto. His eyes widened and pointed his gun to shoot.

The blast from discharging weapons barely covered Joany's screams, along with the crash of glass breaking at the front of the clinic. General Morgan and Kade ran in, guns drawn like it was the O.K. Corral. The general jerked the man on the floor to his feet and found he'd been shot twice, one in the shoulder, which caused him to drop his gun, and another one in the hip. When the general released his grip, Omar collapsed again like a rag doll to the floor.

Vivian continued to aim her Glock at the Afghan, in shock. She glared at the man on the floor until the general shouted at her.

"Dr. Palmer! Put the weapon down. Now!" he ordered.

Her eyes narrowed then shifted her attention to the downed man as the police swarmed in, ready for action with enough firepower to take out a terrorist cell. The general rushed to relieve Vivian of her weapon as Kade knelt to assist Dr. Mac and Joany. The paramedics attended the wounded, along with Vivian and her friends. Rasheed led Vivian out to the parking lot when Kade came barreling out into the open and grabbed her.

"There's a bomb!" Kade slammed her to the ground and covered her with his body as the truck exploded. It set off alarms in all the vehicles, but no one was hurt, thanks to Kade's quick actions. Before he could stand, a burly firemen lifted him off Vivian then assisted Rasheed. One of her legs was twisted, causing him to yell for help.

Kade shook off the firemen and lifted her into his arms, then carried her to the ambulance. "It's going to be okay," he said calmly as he set her down on the step of one of the ambulances.

"Well, hello, hotshot. Long time no see." Vivian grinned. "This all feels really familiar." She tried to stand, but when she wobbled, Kade gathered her in his arms and held on for dear life. Without hesitation, she wrapped her arms around his neck and sobbed into his shoulder.

"Is life always this exciting with you?" Kade held her tight and kissed the side of her head.

"Think you can handle that?" she asked, trying to lean back.

"I intend to make that my goal in life."

"This wasn't how I saw our reunion, Kade. I'm sorry you got caught in this."

"Let's get you checked out and go home. We have a

lot to talk about," he said.

"Kade, I don't think I ever told you, but…"

"I love you, too, Colonel Palmer."

$$\sim\;\sim\;\sim\;\sim$$

One year later

The audience went crazy as Kade Atwood concluded his last show of the season. When he was called out for the second encore, a stagehand brought him a barstool and an acoustic guitar. He motioned for the crowd to settle down. When they were ready, he rested his arm across the guitar.

"Tonight, I'd like for you to meet the love of my life. Mrs. Vivian Atwood. He walked off stage then led her back out. He gripped her hand and kissed her on the lips after helping her sit on the stool. As he rubbed her bulging stomach, he grinned at the audience. "We're expecting our first baby in a couple months. I'd like to name him Mozart since that old boy helped bring us together. But now, I'm going to sing the first song I wrote for her, 'Whiskey and Sweet Tea.' Never take the person you love for granted."

The lights went down with thousands of fans hanging on every word of the song. But for the former Colonel Vivian Palmer and country music star, Kade Atwood, they were the only two people in the building.

MEET THE AUTHOR
Adventure, Thriller & Romantic Suspense Author

Tierney James decided to become a full-time writer after working in education for over thirty years. Besides serving as a Solar System Ambassador for NASA's Jet Propulsion Lab, and attending Space Camp for Educators, Tierney served as a Geo-teacher for National Geographic. Her love of travel and cultures took her on adventures throughout Africa, Asia and Europe. From the Great Wall of China to floating the Okavango Delta of Botswana, Tierney weaves her unique experiences into the adventures she loves to write. Living on a Native American reservation and in a mining town, fuels the characters in the Enigma, Dark Side, and now the Strong Women series. She has now introduced another set of heroes in the Whispers of Angels series.

After moving to Oklahoma, the love of teaching continued in her marketing and writing workshops along with the creation of educational materials and children's books. Try some of her other books to bring a little adventure to your life.

http://www.tierneyjames.com. Speaking at book clubs, school functions, church and community groups are a few of the things Tierney enjoys doing when not writing her next adventure. She also helps beginning writers in their quest to becoming a published author through her workshops and classes. Family, travel and gardening fill her life with plenty of laughter to share with others.

Tierney has been an Amazon #1 Best Selling author and won awards at the Annual Ozark Creative Writer's Conference as well as the Sleuths' Ink Mystery Writers, and Between the Pages Writers' Con.

adventure series that will make you fall in love, while it drives you toward an unexpected conclusion.

The Rescued Heart

Fawn Turnbough returns home in hopes of putting her life back together. Instead, she finds Garrett Horton, the devil in blue jeans who drove her away ten years earlier, waiting to pick up where they left off. Her father, however, is determined to keep them apart. He intends to hide the secret that forced her to run away from the hard rock miner in the first place. He is convinced Garrett only wants Fawn's inheritance and his lead mines.

With a tornado on the ground, headed toward the elementary school, Fawn digs deep to protect those in her care only to put another life in jeopardy. The mine rescue team, shocked at the devastation, races against time to save the children buried in the rubble.

With shattered lives and buried secrets exposed, Garrett discovers sometimes to rescue your dreams you sacrifice a hatred that could threaten everything. He is determined that this time nothing will stop him from taking what he wants most, but will he be able to break the barrier of a heart as hard as the lead he brings up from the mines of the Ozark Mountains?

OTHER TIERNEY JAMES BOOKS

The Enigma Series
An Unlikely Hero
Winds of Deception
Rooftop Angels
Kifaru
Black Mamba
Knight Before Chaos
Invisible Goodbye
Martyrs Never Die
The Hemlock Switch
Knight of the Sugar Plum Fairy
China Dolls

The Dark Side Series
Dark Side of Morning
Dark Side of Noon

Strong Independent Women Series
House of Miracles
The Rescued Heart
Whiskey & Sweet Tea

Whispers of Angels Series
Dance of the Devil's Trill (Prequel)
The Unleashed Miracle

Standalone Books
Turnback Creek
Secrets, Lies & Chocolate Chip Cookies - Cookbook
Lipstick & Danger – Collection of Short Stories
How to Market a Book Someone Besides Your Mother Will Read

Children's Books
There's a Superhero in the Library
Zombie Meatloaf
Mission K9 Rescue